"Destroy him."

Mr. Merrill turned to Doc. "If The Ghost is no longer capable of competing, he has no more value to me. Destroy him."

Val felt as if someone had punched her in the stomach.

"*Destroy* him?" she gasped.

Mr. Merrill didn't look at her. His steely eyes were fixed on Doc. "Put him down, if you prefer. But do it immediately. There's no point in prolonging the life of a horse that will never be an asset to Longmeadow Farm."

Val was trembling so much she could hardly speak. Clutching her father's arm, she whispered, "Dad, you *can't*!"

**Look for these and other Apple Paperbacks
in your local bookstore!**

Animal Inn # 2
A Kid's Best Friend
   by Virginia Vail
Tarantulas on the Brain
   by Marilyn Singer
The Mystery at Peacock Place
   by M.F. Craig
Panky and William
   by Nancy Saxon
Panky in the Saddle
   by Nancy Saxon

ANIMAL INN

PETS ARE FOR KEEPS

Virginia Vail

AN
APPLE
PAPERBACK

SCHOLASTIC INC.
New York Toronto London Auckland Sydney

To my daughter, Amanda, the animal nut.

ISBN 0-590-43434-9

12 11 10 9 8 7 6 5 4 3 2   0 1 2 3 4/9

Printed in the U.S.A.   28

Chapter 1

"Take it easy, Rodney. Don't get all upset. Your leg's going to be just fine, I promise. My dad is the best vet in the world. Don't be nervous."

Valentine Taylor was on her knees talking to a very unhappy beagle in the waiting room of her father's veterinary clinic, Animal Inn. As she stroked the dog's smooth head and silky ears, she looked at Rodney's left hind leg. It was all swollen around a nasty gash, and Val knew that meant the wound was infected. According to Mr. Shue, Rodney's worried master, the beagle had had a run in with a raccoon a few nights ago. Val hoped the raccoon wasn't rabid. She had already checked Rodney's file to make certain he'd had his rabies shot on schedule.

"Come on, Val," said Mr. Shue, shaking his head. "You talk to that dog like he was a person!"

Val looked up at him, her expression serious. "I guess it sounds silly to you, Mr. Shue, but I really think animals understand what we say to them. Maybe not every single word, but I'm absolutely *sure* Rodney knows what I mean. Don't you, boy?" she asked the dog. It drove her best friend, Jill Dearborne, crazy when Val carried on conversations with any animal she happened to meet. Just the day before, Val had chatted with a fat squirrel while she and Jill were waiting for the school bus.

"Honestly, Val, can't you stop talking to birds and squirrels and stray dogs?" Jill had said. "People'll think you're nuts! I swear, if you don't cut that out, I'm going to pretend I don't even *know* you!"

Rodney raised his big brown eyes to meet Val's hazel ones and howled. So far on this particular September Saturday, Rodney was the only patient. Val was grateful for that. Sometimes there were so many sick or injured animals that she didn't have time to give each one individual attention.

Mr. Shue smiled at her. "No, Val, I don't think it's silly. Matter of fact, I talk to Rodney all the time myself. It's like they say — a dog is man's best friend. And you gotta talk to your best friend, right?"

Val smiled back. "Right!"

Just then the door buzzer sounded, and a plump middle-aged woman came in, clutching a huge striped cat in her arms. The cat looked angry.

"Hi, Miss Kleindinst," Val said cheerfully. "Is Pussum here for his shots?"

"That's right," said Miss Kleindinst. "There, there, Pussum, don't pay any attention to the nice doggie.

We'll just sit way over here, and he won't bother you one little bit."

Giving Rodney one last reassuring pat, Val went over to the cat and scratched him under the chin. Pussum responded with a tentative purr.

"That's a neat collar, Pussum," said Val. "I really like the rhinestones."

"Just bought it for him the other day," Miss Kleindinst said proudly. "It was on sale at the Pet Emporium. Three-fifty reduced to a dollar-and-a-half. Will we have to wait long?"

"Not too long," Val told her. "Doc's taking care of Mrs. Myers' Pekingese, Ling-ling. He has an abscessed tooth. Then it's Mr. Shue's turn with Rodney, and you're next."

"Good," said Miss Kleindinst. "Pussum *hates* waiting."

Val wished Miss Kleindinst would break down and buy a cat carrier for Pussum, but she knew that if one wasn't on sale at the Pet Emporium for at least fifty percent off, Miss Kleindinst wouldn't buy it. Pussum, however, was a really finicky cat, and among the many things he hated were dogs. Val hoped there wouldn't be any trouble between the cat and Rodney. It had been such a quiet day at Animal Inn so far.

Val went over to the reception desk, which was separated from the rest of the waiting room by a long, low counter and opened the card file. Doc had a card for each of his regular animal patients with a record of their illnesses, medications and shots. She flipped through the cards and scanned the records of her family's pets. The Taylors had a big orange and white tomcat named Cleveland, as well as two dogs, four hamsters, four rabbits, one canary, and one very fat duck. Luckily, all the animals got along peacefully, at least most of the time. Getting back to business, Val finally found Pussum's card. It had been filed under "P" for Pussum rather than "K" for Kleindinst. Sometimes things could get a little disorganized at Animal Inn.

The phone rang, and Val picked up the receiver. "Hello, Animal Inn. May I help you?" she asked briskly. "A guinea pig? Yes, we treat guinea pigs. What's the matter with him? . . . Oh, sorry — *her.* . . . Sounds like an upper respiratory infection. Could you bring Whistler in on Tuesday around . . . uh . . ." she flipped through Doc's appointment book, ". . . three o'clock? Unless she's very sick. If she is, Doc'll make a house call or you could come in today. . . . Three o'clock Tuesday . . . You're welcome."

Val hung up and glanced into the waiting room, checking to make sure Rodney and Pussum were all right. Though Pussum was growling softly under his breath, Rodney was paying no attention. So far, so good.

Val sat down in the chair behind the reception

desk, enjoying the peace and quiet. Early September sunlight streamed through the windows and glanced off the many framed photographs of Doc's patients that hung on the pine-paneled walls. As always, Val's eyes were drawn to a photo on the back wall. It was a picture of the whole Taylor family: Doc and Mom; Val's younger sister Erin, and little brother Teddy; and their two dogs, Jocko, the little black and white mongrel, and Sunshine, the big golden retriever. They were all smiling into the camera, even the dogs. Val had been ten at the time, Erin eight, and Teddy only five.

Tears suddenly stung Val's eyes. Only three years ago her mother had died in an automobile accident. Right after his wife's death, Doc had been in terrible shape. He'd walked around like a zombie. He hadn't eaten, or even bothered to shave. That was when he'd grown his beard. Val hated it; she thought it made him look old. It was as though Doc had aged ten years — maybe twenty — while he mourned. And Val felt as if she had aged a lot, too. Maybe not visibly, like Doc, but deep inside. It seemed that the pain of losing Mom would never go away. After three years, it hadn't. Maybe it never would.

Val felt much older than thirteen; and because of her height — five-feet-eight-inches — people tended to think she was more mature than she actually was. Erin, eleven now, looked as much like

5

their mother as Val did like their father. Erin was slender, blonde and delicate while Val was tall, auburn-haired and sturdy. More than anything in the world, Erin wanted to be a ballet dancer like their mother, who had danced with the Pennsylvania Ballet before Val was born. Eight-year-old Teddy, Val thought, was a mixture of both parents, solidly built like Doc and Val, but with their mother's fair hair and big blue eyes. Teddy could be a cherub one minute and a mischievous imp the next —

Meeeeeow! Pffft! Sss!

Wooofwooofwooof!

Val leaped from her seat and dashed around the counter into the waiting room. Pussum had launched an all-out attack on the beagle. Miss Kleindinst, taken by surprise, had dropped the leash attached to Pussum's jeweled collar and was squawking at the top of her lungs. "Oh, Pussum! Naughty, naughty! Oh, dear! That horrible *dog* is going to hurt Pussum!"

As for Rodney, he was barking at the top of his lungs. But the barks quickly turned into yelps of pain when Pussum buried his sharp claws in Rodney's tender nose.

"Get that murderin' cat off my dog!" yelled Mr. Shue, tugging on Rodney's leash. "Rodney's *bleeding!*"

Val plunged into the middle of the battle, reaching first for one animal, then the other. Pussum, wild-

6

eyed, sprang across the room and zipped under a bench. Rodney was straining so hard against his leash that he could only let out a series of strangled yelps. On her hands and knees, Val tried to drag Pussum out of his hiding place, while ducking to avoid his sharp claws. She finally latched onto one furry foreleg, murmuring soft, soothing words; but Pussum was beyond being soothed. Now that Rodney was out of his reach, the cat switched his attack to Val and raked her arm with his claws, hissing and spitting. Val gritted her teeth and finally succeeded in getting a firm grip on Pussum and hauling him out from under the bench.

"Calm down, Pussum. It's okay," she muttered, stroking the cat's ruffled fur. Pussum continued to growl under his breath as Val returned him to Miss Kleindinst.

"Poor, poor pussycat!" Miss Kleindinst crooned. "Did that big, nasty dog scare you to death?"

"Big nasty dog, my foot!" Mr. Shue grumbled. "That cat's a menace. Ain't you got a box to put it in? Wild animals like that oughtn't run around loose. Just look what it did to Rodney!"

"Let me take a look at Rodney's nose, Mr. Shue," Val offered, dabbing at her injured arm. Her scratch wasn't deep, but it was bleeding. Good thing Doc had insisted that she have a tetanus shot before she started working at Animal Inn. She'd swab her wound with hydrogen peroxide. And she'd better put some on Rodney's nose, too.

Just then the phone rang again.

Val dashed to pick it up. "I'll be with you in a minute, Mr. Shue. Here — " she grabbed a fistful of tissues from a box on the desk and thrust them at him. "Mop him off with this . . . OH!"

In the commotion, Val hadn't noticed the arrival of still another pet owner, and she'd just tripped over a pair of very large sneakered feet. They belonged to a tall, gangly boy about Val's own age with a mop of thick brown hair and a broad grin. He was holding a pet carrier in one big hand.

Not another cat! Val groaned inwardly. At least it was safely enclosed, unlike Pussum.

"*Pussum!*" Val wailed as the cat made one last desperate bid for freedom, leaping out of Miss Kleindinst's tender embrace.

"You get the phone — I'll get the cat," said the boy cheerfully, putting the carrier down on the counter. He was just in time to grab Pussum's tail with one hand and scoop up the cat with the other, tucking him gently but firmly under his arm.

"Thanks!" cried Val, snatching up the receiver. "Hello — Innimal Ann . . . I mean, Animal Inn! . . . Well, if it's not an emergency, maybe you ought to come in a little later. . . . Yes, I remember Killer, your Doberman. If it's only for a checkup and shots,

8

could you wait until next week? . . . Yes, I'll put him down for two o'clock Thursday. Bye!"

She hung up, entered Killer in Doc's appointment book for Thursday afternoon, then found the bottle of peroxide and patted some of her scratch with a wad of sterile cotton.

"Looks like the beagle could use some of that," said the boy, stretching out a hand. "What happened to you? Cat attack?"

Val nodded ruefully and handed him the bottle and some more cotton. Pussum had once again been returned to his owner, looking innocent and smug, and was snuggled down in Miss Kleindinst's lap. Rodney was whimpering sadly, cowering next to Mr. Shue. "Thanks for your help," Val said to the boy.

Just then Doc stuck his head out of the treatment room to say, "Everything all right, Vallie? I heard a lot of commotion. . . ."

"Everything's fine, Dad," Val assured him quickly. "Pussum and Rodney got into a fight, but it's all over now."

Doc Taylor, dressed like Val in jeans and T-shirt under his white coat, wore scuffed Nikes on his big feet, and a stethoscope around his neck. He glanced over at Rodney and Pussum, and frowned.

"Miss Kleindinst, it's high time you got a carrier for Pussum. I can't have him attacking my other patients every time he comes into the office."

Miss Kleindinst looked embarrassed. "I know, Doc. The very next time they go on sale at the Pet Emporium I'm going to buy one. But what can you expect when Pussum sees a dog? Cats and dogs are natural enemies, and that dog is mean!"

Mr. Shue scowled. "Rodney's not mean. He was minding his own business when that killer cat — "

"Miss Kleindinst, please get a carrier, all right?" Doc turned to Val. "I'll be finished with Ling-ling in a few minutes. Who's next, Vallie?"

"Mr. Shue and Rodney. I'm sorry about the fight, Dad. I should have been paying more attention," said Val.

"You're doing fine, honey. Don't know what I'd do without you." Doc gave her a warm smile as he went back into the treatment room.

Val noticed that the boy had finished tending to Rodney's nose, and was now hunkered down next to the beagle. He was deep in a discussion with Mr. Shue about the merits of beagles and other hunting dogs. Mr. Shue seemed to have gotten over his anger at Miss Kleindinst and her cat; as for Pussum, he was sound asleep.

Since everything appeared to be under control for the moment, Val bent down and peered into the carrier the boy had left on the counter. She was surprised to see not another cat but a gray rabbit with a busily twitching pink nose.

"Hi, fella. What's your problem?" she asked.

"We're not sure what's wrong with him. That's why I brought him in," the boy said. "His name's Harvey. Mine's Toby — Toby Curran. You're Doc Taylor's daughter, right?"

Val nodded. "Yes. My name's Valentine, but everyone calls me Val. Guess I'd better make out a card for Harvey, since he's never been here before."

Toby waited while Val seated herself behind the desk, pulled out a blank index card, and printed neatly, "Harvey Curran."

"How old is Harvey?" she asked in her best professional manner.

"About six months old, I guess. I'm not quite sure. He's my brother's rabbit — my kid brother Jake, that is. He's real worried about Harvey lately — says he hasn't been eating right. . . ."

Before Toby could say more, the front door of Animal Inn burst open. A plump and frantic elderly lady strode in, struggling with the weight of a huge cat carrier.

"Mrs. Wentworth, what's the matter?" asked Val, jumping up from her chair.

"We have to see the doctor immediately!" cried Mrs. Wentworth. "We're having kittens!"

Mrs. Wentworth was the proud owner of a prize-winning Siamese cat, Princess Tuptim. She considered the welfare of her pet much more important than that of any of Doc's other patients. The Princess was expecting her first litter, and Mrs. Wentworth had been on the phone with Doc every single day to report on the cat's progress. Doc had assured her that Tuptim would know what to do when the time came. But now, here she was, with Tuptim yowling from inside the carrier. Tuptim was probably furious, Val thought, at having been dragged away from her comfortable home.

Val hurried around the counter. "Gee, Mrs. Wentworth, that's great! But why did you bring her here? Doc told you that everything was fine and Tuptim wasn't going to have any trouble."

"But she *is* having trouble," Mrs. Wentworth wailed. "She's in terrible pain! Just listen to her!"

Yeeeooooow! Tuptim yelled.

"She's probably unhappy because she's being jiggled around," Val suggested. "When cats are going to have kittens, they like to hide away somewhere quiet, and to be left alone."

"That's silly!" Mrs. Wentworth snapped. "Now you run and tell your father to come out here right this minute!"

"He's taking care of an abscessed tooth, Mrs. Wentworth," Val explained. "Why don't you just sit down here for a minute and let me take a look at Tuptim?"

"Oh, dear, oh, dear! What am I going to do?

She's going to die, I know she is!" Mrs. Wentworth was practically in tears. Val knew that irritating as Mrs. Wentworth often was, she truly loved her cat.

Val squatted down beside the carrier, opened the lid, and looked in at Tuptim. The cat was obviously in labor. Tuptim's slightly crossed turquoise-blue eyes gazed up at Val beseechingly, and Val stroked her pale cream-colored fur. "She's not going to die, Mrs. Wentworth. It's like Doc told you — she's a perfectly healthy cat, and she's going to have perfectly beautiful kittens. . . . Well, what do you know! Here's the first one now!" Val beamed in delight as a tiny ball of wet fur made its first appearance. No matter how many times she saw baby animals born, Val always felt a special joy and awe when it happened again.

Mrs. Wentworth covered her eyes with her hands. "Oh, no, what should we do? Call your father at once!"

"It's okay, Tuptim knows exactly what to do," Val pointed out gently. "See? She's licking it now. She'll probably have about four more. I'll buzz Doc and tell him what's happening, but Tuptim doesn't need any help. She's doing just fine!"

"She sure is," Toby put in, leaning over Val's shoulder to look at the newborn kitten. "We have lots of cats on our farm, and all of them were born without any help from us."

"Nothing to worry about," Miss Kleindinst added, holding Pussum who had just woken and was very interested in what was going on. "Cats are tough — even fancy cats like that one."

Val went to the phone and pressed the intercom button.

"Dad, Mrs. Wentworth is here with Tuptim. Tuptim's had her first kitten, and everything's okay, but Mrs. Wentworth would like you to take over as soon as you can."

"Be there in a minute. Hang in there, Vallie," came Doc's voice over the speaker.

A moment later, Doc came out of the treatment room and smiled broadly at Mrs. Wentworth. "Congratulations!" he said. "One down and about four more to go, I'd say. Look at that little fella! Tuptim's a born mother. In a little while you're going to be the proud owner of a litter of beautiful Siamese kittens!"

"Oh, Doc, you really think so? And Princess Tuptim is going to be all right, isn't she?" Mrs. Wentworth swallowed hard. "It's not important that she's a champion. What's *really* important is that she'll be all right. If I lost Tuptim, I — I don't know what I'd do. . . ." She wiped her eyes with a lace-edged handkerchief.

"I promise you that Tuptim will be absolutely fine. I know how difficult it is for you to go through all this, so you just go home and take it easy. I'll call you when the last kitten is born so you can open a bottle of champagne and toast the occasion," Doc said.

Mrs. Wentworth smiled through her tears. "Oh, Doc, if you say so, I guess I have to take your word. Thank you — and thank *you*, Val. I didn't mean to be abrupt with you. It's just that Princess Tuptim is . . . well, she's very special to me. I'd be so lonely without her. . . ."

Doc escorted Mrs. Wentworth to her car while Val took Tuptim and her first kitten into the infirmary. When she came back into the waiting room, she found Toby standing by Harvey's carrier. Time to pick up where she'd left off.

"Mr. Shue and Rodney are next, Dad," she said as her father came back in. After Doc, Mr. Shue, and the beagle had gone into the treatment room, she picked up Harvey's card.

"Tell me more about Harvey's problem," she said.

"Well, the other day he started pulling out his fur," said Toby. "Jake's afraid he'll end up bald. And he's afraid that whatever Harvey's got, Henry will catch — Henry's his other rabbit."

"Funny — he doesn't look sick, just kind of mangy. And he sure is fat for an animal who's off his feed. . . . Hey, wait a minute!" Val suddenly put two and two together. "You say he's been pulling out his fur?"

Toby nodded.

Val stifled a giggle. "I'm pretty sure that Henry couldn't possibly catch what Harvey's got!"

"You mean you know what's wrong with him?" Toby asked hopefully.

Val said solemnly, "Yes, I think I do."

"Is it serious? I mean, he's not gonna die or anything, is he?"

Val shook her head. "You might say it's serious, but it's perfectly natural," she said with a grin.

Toby scowled. "What's so funny? A sick animal's nothing to laugh about!"

"You're absolutely right," Val said. "But Harvey's not sick. Like I said, it's perfectly natural. Harvey's pregnant!"

"You're kidding! You're crazy!" Toby blustered. He quickly added, "Hey, I'm sorry. I didn't mean to be rude, but you have to be mistaken. It isn't possible — Harvey's a boy!"

"I'd bet this week's salary that he's not," said Val. "And I'd bet next week's salary that Henry *is*! I've had rabbits for years, and I've read all about them in my father's medical books. Rabbits pull out their fur to make a soft nest for their babies when they're born. Their gestation period is from thirty to thirty-five days. . . . Do you know what 'gestation' is?"

"What do you think I am — stupid?" Toby snapped. "My dad owns Curran's Dairy. I know all about cows, and I know that gestation means the time from when an animal gets pregnant until she calves."

"Kindles," Val said smugly.

"Kindles?"

"When cows have babies, they calve. When rabbits have babies, it's called kindling. The doe starts making her nest about a week before she kindles, so I'd say that Harvey's going to become a mother within the next few days."

"No way," Toby said flatly. "I'm going to wait and see what Doc Taylor says."

"Do you want to bet?" Val asked, annoyed at his superior attitude.

"Bet what?"

"I said I'd bet a week's salary that Harvey's going to have babies. And I never bet unless I'm one hundred percent sure!"

"You're on," Toby said immediately. "I don't have a whole lot of money, but I'll take the bet anyway. And if I lose — " (his tone implied that it was highly unlikely) " — I'll work for your dad here at Animal Inn for two weeks for free. Okay?"

"Okay!" Val turned away to answer the phone. Toby, his rather prominent ears bright pink, snatched Harvey's carrier and stamped over to a vacant chair in the waiting room.

"Good afternoon, Animal Inn," Val chirped into the receiver. What a pig-headed boy! she thought as she listened to the person who was calling, automatically making notes on the message pad. I almost wish I was wrong. I'm not sure it's a great idea to have him around here for two whole weeks!

"Yes, Mr. Merrill, I've got it. Yes, I'll make sure that Doc gets the message. . . . No, he can't come to the phone right now. He's busy with a patient. . . . Just as soon as he's available. Yes, I'll repeat the message: Your horse, The Gray Ghost, has had an accident and you're afraid his right foreleg is fractured. . . . All right, Mr. Merrill, I've got it all down. . . . You want me to repeat it *again*?" Val frowned at the receiver. "Okay, here goes. The Gray Ghost, your championship jumper, crashed through a five-bar gate in your ring at Longmeadow Farms, and the vet who usually attends him is out of town, so will Dr. Taylor please come to Longmeadow as soon as possible and you'll make it worth his while. . . . No, Mr. Merrill, I don't think he can leave his other patients to come right now. . . . Of course I'll tell him right away. Good-bye, Mr. Merrill."

As she hung up, Val felt sad. Longmeadow's

Gray Ghost was so beautiful and famous. He'd been winning prizes in the show ring as long as Val could remember, and every triumph had been recorded in the local newspaper. The Gray Ghost was probably the most famous animal in Essex, Pennsylvania! She wished Doc *could* go out there right away, but of course all the other pet owners considered their animals just as important. And so did Doc, Val knew.

Mr. Shue and Rodney came out of the treatment room. Rodney had a big bandage on his leg, and was happily wagging his tail. Val relayed Mr. Merrill's message, word for word, to her father.

"Thank you, Vallie," Doc said. "All right, Miss Kleindinst. You can bring Pussum in now." He looked over at Val and grinned. "Tuptim's had another kitten, and it's a beauty!"

Chapter
2

"Well, young man," Doc Taylor said to Toby some time later, having given Harvey a brief examination. "I hope your brother has a large hutch, because he's going to have a lot of rabbits in a few days."

"Holy cow!" Toby said. "Harvey really *is* a girl! Boy, is Jake gonna be surprised!"

It was all Val could do not to say, "I told you so," but she didn't. She just concentrated on soothing poor nervous Harvey, who was trembling in her arms, pink nose twitching faster than ever. She couldn't help smiling a little, and, when she glanced up at Toby, he smiled, too.

"Guess you won the bet," he said ruefully.

"Guess I did," Val said.

Doc looked from one to the other. "Did I miss something? What bet?"

"Well, sir," Toby said, reaching out to stroke one of Harvey's long, quivering ears, "your daughter told me Harvey was pregnant, but I didn't believe her, and she bet me a week's salary she was right, so I took her up on it. Only I can't pay up, so I said I'd work here at Animal Inn for two weeks for free. . . . Guess I ought to have checked with you first, huh?''

Val noticed that Toby's ears were turning red again — with embarrassment this time — so she said quickly, "We could really use some more help, Dad. And Toby's very good with animals. He got Rodney all calmed down and Mr. Shue, too, after Pussum ripped up Rodney's nose. Maybe he could help out when I'm not here, after school.'' She turned to Toby. "You don't go to Hamilton, do you?''

Val was in the eighth grade at Alexander Hamilton Junior High. She knew just about everybody in her school, and she was sure she'd never seen Toby before.

"No, our farm is outside the town limits, so I go to Kennedy,'' Toby said. "I'm on the ninth-grade basketball team — the Buffalos. We were state champions last year. Usually after school I help my dad with the cows, but maybe I could come here two or three days a week.''

Doc Taylor nodded. "Well, Toby, as far as I'm concerned, it's all right with me, your working here. But I don't think it's quite fair for you not to be paid. Maybe we could work something out.''

Toby cut in, "Oh, no Dr. Taylor. I made a

bet, and I lost. But maybe, after I've worked here for two weeks and you think you could use me — if I do all right, that is — and if you really need somebody . . . well, maybe then. . . ."

"Whatever you say." Doc Taylor began washing his hands at the little sink in the treatment room. "You're right. A bet is a bet." He glanced at Val and grinned. "But I imagine you've learned not to argue with Vallie as far as animals are concerned. Her diagnoses are usually pretty accurate. When she grows up, she's going to be a better veterinarian than I am!"

Val blushed. "Oh, come on, Dad! If I could be half as good as you, I'd be happy."

"Any more patients, Vallie?" Doc asked.

"Only one. I told you that Mr. Merrill called from Longmeadow about The Gray Ghost." Val put Harvey back into her carrier and latched the door. "Guess we better get over there and see what's happening."

Doc grimaced. "Yes, I suppose we should. And maybe we could drop off Toby on the way. Longmeadow is near your father's farm, right?" he asked.

"That's right. I was going to take the bus, but if you're going my way. . . ."

"We'll give you a lift. Put Harvey in the back of the van, and we'll get going just as soon as we clean this place up a little." Doc looked at Toby. "If you're serious about working here, how about getting

22

a broom and sweeping out the waiting room? When Mike gets here, he'll do the heavy cleaning."

"Who's Mike?" Toby asked.

"Mike Strickler," Doc said. "He's our night watchman and janitor. He also takes care of the animals in the infirmary after hours — a real jack-of-all-trades."

"Did I just hear my name taken in vain?"

A short, spry-looking man stuck his head in the door at that moment. His bright blue eyes fastened on Toby. "Hey, you're one of Bill Curran's boys, ain'tcha? Sure y'are! Look just like your pop — known him since before you was born. Knew your grandpop, too. Fine man, fine man. Hiya, Val. How ya doing? Well, Doc, I'm waiting. Don't have all day to stand around gabbin'. Got work to do!"

As Doc Taylor walked with Mike into the infirmary, Val showed Toby where to find the broom, then she began swabbing down the table in the treatment room with disinfectant. She couldn't help smiling. Mike always seemed like a Pennsylvania Dutch leprechaun to her. Of course, she knew there wasn't any such thing, but if there were, she was sure he'd look just like Mike.

"What a funny old guy!" Toby said, as he swept. "He sure talks a lot. Is he always that way?"

"Always," Val said. "During the day he hangs around Stetler's Grain and Feed Store, talking to

23

everybody who comes in. He knows absolutely everybody in Essex — all the farmers, anyway. And I bet when he's here alone at night, he talks to the animals." Like me, she thought, but didn't say. Toby'd probably laugh.

A few minutes later, Doc returned.

"Mike's having a serious conversation with Ling-ling," he told Val and Toby with a twinkle, "comparing notes on dental care. It seems Mike had an abscessed tooth pulled recently, just like Ling-ling." He looked around the office. "Well, are we all squared away here?" Toby and Val nodded. "Then let's go. Onward and upward to the green pastures of Long-meadow!"

A few miles out of town, Doc turned Animal Inn's van into a private lane between two stone pillars on which twin brass plaques proclaimed LONG-MEADOW FARMS. A sign beside one of the pillars warned, PRIVATE PROPERTY. TRESPASSERS WILL BE PROSECUTED.

"Friendly little place, isn't it?" said Toby, peering out the window at the green rolling acres surrounded by white-painted rail fences. The lane was bordered with tall trees whose branches met overhead, forming a shadowed green tunnel, and at the end of it was the home of Mr. Trevor Merrill. On the trip over, Toby had made it clear that he was very curious to see the Merrill place, which he'd heard

24

so much about. So Doc had agreed to take him home on the way back from Longmeadow, rather than dropping him off on the way. Harvey, snugly tucked away in her carrier in the back of the van, had made no objection.

Val was sitting on the edge of her seat with excitement. Of all the animals she loved, she loved horses most. One of her earliest dreams had been to have a horse of her own, but as their housekeeper, Mrs. Racer, often said, "If wishes were horses, beggars would ride." And Val's wish had never come true. Doc and her mother had taken her to many horse shows in Harrisburg, though. She had held her breath during the jumping events, and year after year Longmeadow's Gray Ghost had won first prize.

How old must The Ghost be now? Val wondered. For a long time, he'd been listed on the horse show programs as "aged," meaning that he was over ten. But he was still the best; he'd even won at Madison Square Garden three years earlier. Now this beautiful, famous horse had injured his leg. Val only hoped that it wasn't really broken. If it was, considering his age, his career as a champion would be over. Maybe he'd just pulled a tendon. But how could a jumper as experienced as The Ghost have misjudged a jump so badly? Val just couldn't believe it was his fault. Perhaps whoever was riding him at the time hadn't given him the proper signals, or something had spooked him at the last minute.

Val had taken a few riding lessons when she was younger and now she sometimes rode at The Barn, a local riding stable. But she had never learned to jump. She did not have enough riding experience for that, and The Barn's horses were not champion jumpers. She had also studied enough horse anatomy to know how serious it could be for a jumper to fracture the front cannon bone. Oh, poor Ghost!

The van pulled to a stop in a semi-circular drive in front of a Georgian-style mansion of rosy brick, with tall white columns and a spacious veranda. It looked just like a plantation house in old Virginia. Boxwood hedges surrounded the drive, and Val could imagine the beautiful gardens that must lie somewhere out of sight.

"Wonder where the stables are?" said Doc.

"Maybe he could tell us," Toby offered, as a man in slacks and a pink polo shirt appeared in the doorway and hurried down the steps that led to the drive. He had sleek brown hair, a bristly mustache, and a frown on his tanned forehead. He strode over to the van and peered inside.

"Dr. Taylor?"

Doc nodded.

"I'm Trevor Merrill. Took you long enough to get here!"

"I believe my daughter told you I was attending to my patients and would come as soon as I could," replied Doc calmly. "So here I am. Where's the horse?"

Merrill's frown did not go away. "Follow that road over to your left. It goes directly to the stables. I'll meet you there." He turned abruptly away and headed for a big silver car parked nearby.

"Friendly kind of guy, isn't he?" said Toby cheerfully. "Nice house, though. And nice car. Must be nice to be so rich!"

Val said nothing. She'd taken an instant dislike to Mr. Merrill. Why should he talk to her father as though he were some kind of servant? Just because the Merrills were the wealthiest family in Essex didn't give Trevor Merrill the right to order people around. Val hoped Doc would charge extra for taking care of The Ghost, but she knew he wouldn't. Doc never charged as much as his services were worth. Sometimes, if people were poor, he didn't charge them anything at all. Some of the owners of his patients paid him in produce from their farms if they couldn't pay him in cash. But Mr. Merrill could afford the best of everything, including veterinary care for his horses.

Val thought about Toby. Doc hadn't even told Toby how much his examination of Harvey would cost. Knowing Doc, she figured he'd never get around to billing the Currans. Toby was just a kid, not a successful stockbroker like Trevor Merrill, so that was okay.

Doc revved up the engine, and a few minutes later the van arrived at Longmeadow's stables. A slender blonde girl was sitting on the white rail fence surrounding the paddock. She was wearing fawn-colored riding breeches above shining leather boots, and her hands were clenched between her knees.

As the van stopped, she raised her head. She was probably about sixteen, Val guessed, and very pretty. When Mr. Merrill's car screeched to a stop right behind the van, the girl slid off the fence and walked slowly over, her head hanging.

"It wasn't my *fault*, Dad," she whined as Mr. Merrill got out. "I just couldn't control him! He went at that fence too fast. It wasn't my fault!"

Doc got out, carrying his black bag, and Toby and Val scrambled after him.

"Where's the patient?" Doc asked.

"I'll show you," said the girl sullenly, scuffing through the dust to the stable. "Third box on the left. His name's on the door."

"*Sean!*" Mr. Merrill bellowed, bustling along behind Doc. "Sean, where are you? You were supposed to be in charge. Tell the doctor what happened."

A small, wiry man who looked like an ex-jockey came out of the tack room.

"Well, Mr. Merrill, sir, it was like this. Miss Cassandra told me you said it was all right for her to take The Ghost over the jumps. I wanted to call you — I *intended* to call you just to make sure — but she said saddle him up, so I saddled him up. And then she took him out onto the course, and I told her to take it easy, didn't I, Miss Cassandra? I mean, I wasn't sure she could handle him, but she said she knew what she was doing, so . . . well, I let her do it. And then . . . well, then. . . ."

"Then *what*?" Mr. Merrill bellowed. Cassandra hung back, scuffing the toe of one boot in the dust.

"Then she started galloping The Ghost, and I yelled at her to slow down. But I guess she didn't hear me or something, so she kept right on going. And then it was like she couldn't control him, and he took off for that five-bar gate, only it was too late. And he didn't make it, and he fell, and she fell off him, only to the side, like, and — "

" — And it's lucky he didn't roll on me and *kill* me!" cried Cassandra. Val noticed that the girl had suddenly developed a pitiful limp. "Don't you care about *me*?" Cassandra wailed. "I could have been *killed*!"

Val and Toby joined the procession into the stable behind Sean and Doc, closely followed by Mr. Merrill, and a reluctant Cassandra. Val's eyes widened as they entered. She'd never seen anything like it before. The box stalls were all of polished wood, and on the door of each was a shiny brass plaque with the horse's name engraved on it. Soft music filled the air, and the whole place smelled sweetly of fresh grain and hay.

"Wow!" Val breathed.

Toby wasn't so easily impressed "This isn't such a big deal," he said. "You should see my dad's dairy barn. Clean as a whistle — and we have music, too."

"You do?' Val asked.

"Sure. Somebody figured out that cows give more milk when they listen to soft music, kind of like the stuff they play in dentists' offices. If you know so much about animals, you oughta know that."

What a know-it-all, Val thought. But before she could think of a response, Sean and Doc had halted before one of the stalls, and her heartbeat quickened. She was about to come face to face with Longmeadow's Gray Ghost, champion jumper and grand old man of the horse-show circuit, whose triumphs she'd applauded so many times in the show ring!

Doc entered The Ghost's stall and Val slipped in beside him.

She'd forgotten how big The Ghost was! He was at least seventeen hands high, which meant that his back was about the same height as the top of Val's head. His dappled coat gleamed in the subdued lighting. But his head was hanging, and his right front leg was swollen and slightly raised from the bed of squeaky-clean straw. Both knees were badly scraped, though someone obviously had cleaned the wounds with antiseptic.

Oh, poor Ghost, Val thought. The last time she'd seen The Ghost was at a horse show. He'd flown over a water jump, ears forward, nostrils flaring, like Pegasus, the mythical winged horse. The audience had gasped in unison, then broken into spontaneous cheers and applause.

And now, just look at him!

Very gently, Doc stroked the big gray gelding's nose. Val could see the pain in the horse's huge brown eyes.

"Daddy, I *told* you it wasn't my fault!" Cassandra wailed. "He's getting too old. He should have *known*. . . ."

Val could cheerfully have killed Cassandra just then. She clenched her fists at her sides.

"Be quiet, Cassandra!" snapped Mr. Merrill. "You had no business trying to take him over that gate. But we'll discuss that later. Dr. Taylor," he said, turning to Doc, "I can't stress strongly enough what this horse's health is worth to me. He's won thousands of dollars in prize money in horse shows all up and down the East Coast, not to mention a roomful of trophies and championship ribbons. Longmeadow's Gray Ghost has had a long and distinguished career. And I didn't intend for his career to end for many years yet. I'm counting on you to make sure that it continues."

Val held The Ghost's halter, murmuring softly to him as Doc began gently feeling his right foreleg. The horse nickered and danced around at the pressure, but Val kept on talking to him, and he soon calmed down once more.

"It might be a hairline fracture of the metacarpus," said Doc. "But I won't be able to tell for sure until I take an x-ray. In the meantime, I'll give him a shot to relieve the pain."

Val hurried to prepare the hypodermic, with a hand that trembled slightly. It was as though she could feel the pain the big gray horse was suffering. As Doc plunged the needle into the gelding's flesh, Val winced, pressing her cheek to The Ghost's and stroking his velvety nose, gentling him as he snorted and tried to jerk away.

"It's all right," she whispered into his ear, rubbing his forelock. "Doc only wants to help you. You're going to be okay, honest. The pain will go away in a few minutes."

The Gray Ghost snorted again and tossed his

head, then calmed down under Val's soothing hands, though his silver tail still switched.

"If you can bring him to Animal Inn, I'll x-ray him immediately," Doc told Mr. Merrill. "But I have to warn you, if it's a fracture, it's going to take a long time to heal. Like people, horses' bones don't knit as quickly when they're past a certain age. How old is The Ghost?"

"Fifteen," said Mr. Merrill. "Past his prime, I know. Sean, tell Willie to bring out the small trailer. He's to drive The Ghost immediately to . . . what did you say the name of your place was?" he asked Doc.

"Animal Inn. It's on Orchard Lane, right off the York road," Doc told him. "I'll meet you there. Is there a phone I can use?"

"In the tack room," said Mr. Merrill.

After a final pat on The Ghost's withers, Doc left the stall, telling Val over his shoulder, "I'm going to call home and tell the kids we'll be later than I thought."

Val nodded, still absorbed in The Ghost. He seemed to like the way she was rubbing between his ears. Reluctantly she turned him over to Sean and followed her father. Toby joined her as she headed for the van.

Mr. Merrill, with a sullen Cassandra at his side,

33

marched out of the stable and got into the silver car.

"Call me with the results of the x-ray immediately," he said to Doc. "I hope you realize that in peak condition this is a very valuable horse."

"All life is valuable, Mr. Merrill," Doc said quietly. He turned into the entrance to the tack room.

A moment later, Mr. Merrill's car purred out of the stable yard and disappeared in a cloud of dust along the road to the Merrill mansion.

Chapter
3

After dropping Toby at the Curran farm, Val and Doc drove back to Animal Inn. They arrived only a few minutes before the Longmeadow horse trailer pulled up. Val directed Willie to the big white-painted barn to the rear of the Small Animal Clinic, where Doc treated horses and farm animals. It certainly wasn't as fancy as Longmeadow's stables, but Val wasn't ashamed of it. She herself had planted the bright red geraniums that bloomed in big wooden tubs on either side of the main entrance.

After giving The Ghost an affectionate pat, Willie took off again, shaking his head sadly and muttering, "That girl shouldn't have given him his head that way. Thinks she knows how to ride, but she doesn't. Where's her brains, I'd like to know?"

As Val and Doc were leading the horse into the examining room, a swallow suddenly darted down from the rafters above, swooping for the open door. The bird passed so close to Val's head that she ducked, but The Ghost paid no attention at all. Val thought

35

that was very strange. So did Doc. He peered intently at the horse's right eye, then at the left. Then he pulled the bandanna he always carried out of the hip pocket of his jeans and waved it in front of The Ghost's right eye.

No reaction.

"Dad," Val whispered, "he didn't *see* it!"

Doc didn't say a word, only moved to the other side of the horse and did the same thing. This time The Ghost tossed his head and fidgeted a little.

"He saw *that*," said Doc, "but not clearly. Vallie, the first thing we do is take an x-ray of that leg, and then I'll examine his eyes very carefully. And I think I know what I'll find. I'm willing to bet that The Ghost is developing cataracts."

"He's going blind?" cried Val. "Oh, Dad, how awful!"

"He's not blind yet, not entirely. But his vision has definitely been impaired. That would explain why a champion like this fellow misjudged that jump. Come on, Vallie. Let's check him out."

It was almost seven o'clock by the time Val and Doc pulled into the driveway of their home, a two-hundred-year-old farmhouse on the outskirts of Essex, Pennsylvania. Dusk was falling, and crickets and locusts, the last diehards of summer, were scraping and chirping their distinctive melodies. Val slid out of the passenger seat of Doc's car, her shoulders hunched in depression. The x-ray had revealed no fracture; a tendon had been pulled, but that would heal fairly rapidly with rest and care. Doc's examination of The Ghost's eyes, however, had confirmed his suspicion that the horse had lost most of the vision in his right eye, and was beginning to lose the vision in his left. Doc had called Mr. Merrill at Longmeadow, but Mr. Merrill was out. He had left a message with the servant who answered the phone for Mr. Merrill to call back in the morning.

"Will he ever be able to jump again?" had been Val's first question, and Doc had told her no. But that didn't mean he'd never walk or trot or canter again. The Ghost had earned the right to retire from the show ring. He'd never be forgotten by anyone who had ever seen him compete. But Val's heart still ached for the big, beautiful animal.

"We ate already," Teddy informed Val and Doc as they came into the big, rambling old stone house. "Mrs. Racer made pork chops with apples, just the way you like 'em, Dad. Hey, Val, wanna hear some funny jokes? My friend Eric gave me this book. . . ."

Teddy's sparkling blue eyes were shadowed by the Phillies baseball cap he always wore. The T-shirt he was wearing, a tattered yellow one that Val had discarded months earlier, completely concealed his shorts, and he had jammed his bare feet into a pair

37

of high-top sneakers with dirty, straggling laces.

"And I did all my homework, honest I did!"

Doc caught Teddy up in a big bear-hug, swinging him around the hall and making him squeal with delight.

"Daddy, Val, guess what!" Erin burst into the hall in leotard and ballet practice shoes, her silvery-blonde hair neatly twisted up in a ballerina knot. "Today in ballet class Miss Tamara told us there's going to be a production of *The Nutcracker* at Christmas, and auditions are next Saturday! And I'm going to try out for the Sugarplum Fairy! I'm almost positive I'll get it, too. I started practicing the minute I got home from class. I already know most of the steps. And when I'm the Sugarplum Fairy, I'll wear Mommy's tiara, the one she wore when she danced it with the Pennsylvania Ballet before you were married, Daddy, remember?"

Doc nodded. "Yes, Erin. I remember. That was the first time I ever saw your mother. She was the most beautiful thing I'd ever laid eyes on."

"That's great, Erin," said Val enthusiastically.

"Wonderful, honey," Doc added, putting Teddy down and giving Erin a hug and a kiss.

Teddy wrinkled his nose. "Whoever heard of a fat fairy?"

"I am *not* fat, Teddy Taylor!" cried Erin, scowling at her little brother.

"Well, *you're* always saying you are," Teddy said. "You keep looking at yourself in the mirror and sucking in your gut. . . ."

"Stomach," Doc corrected.

"Okay, stomach, then. And when you do all those jumps in the living room, the whole *house* shakes!"

"Daddy, make him stop!" cried Erin. "You're such a *pest!*" she said to Teddy.

"That's enough, Teddy," said Doc firmly. "Did you say there are some pork chops left? Sounds good to me. I'm starved."

"Plenty of pork chops," said Mrs. Racer, the Taylors' housekeeper, coming into the hall from the kitchen. She was followed by the two dogs, Jocko and Sunshine. As Val and Doc went into the living room, greeting the dogs, Mrs. Racer removed her spotless white apron and folded it neatly. She was a thin, wiry woman in her late sixties. Her gray hair was severely pulled back under a white lawn cap she called a prayer covering, and she was wearing a simply cut lavender print dress. Mrs. Racer was a Mennonite from the Pennsylvania Dutch country. Val knew that the Mennonites were kind of like the Amish, who were called the "plain people," and lived just the way they had for hundreds of years — no television or any other modern appliances were permitted in their homes or on their farms. Unlike the Amish, however, the Mennonites drove cars, and sent their children to the local schools. And Mrs. Racer loved to watch TV at the Taylors' whenever she had time.

If it hadn't been for Mrs. Racer, the family would have had an even harder time adjusting to Mrs. Taylor's death. Mrs. Racer had been the one to keep the house running and the family going during those first hard months.

"I made toasted cheese sandwiches for you, Vallie," Mrs. Racer told her. Val always felt a little guilty that special food had to be prepared for her, since she didn't eat meat. But she loved animals so much that she just couldn't stand the thought of eating them, and Mrs. Racer and Doc both understood.

"Thanks, Mrs. Racer," said Val. "I just love toasted cheese!"

"Put them in the microwave for a few minutes and they'll be nice and hot," Mrs. Racer added. She peered up at Doc.

"Doc, you look all worn out. That horse give you a lot of trouble?"

Doc smiled. "Not much. It was a long day, that's all. Don't know how I would have managed without my trusty assistant here."

Val felt proud. Her father's words of praise always made her feel good, even when she was tired and sad, like now. She flopped down in a big, worn armchair and frowned. Something was missing.

Cleveland. Where was her big fat orange cat? Usually he outraced the dogs to welcome her home, but he was nowhere in sight.

"Where's Cleveland?" she asked, looking around the room.

"I'll get him," said Teddy, and dashed off. He returned a moment later, his arms overflowing with twelve pounds of cat.

"Oh, Cleveland!" Val sighed, as Teddy dumped him on her lap. "Not again!"

Cleveland's broad pink nose was badly scratched. It was obvious that he'd been in another fight.

"Cleveland, what's the matter with you?" Val asked the cat sternly, examining the scratch. "Don't you know that house cats aren't supposed to get into fights?"

"It was the Millers' horrible gray tom again," Erin informed her, perching on the arm of Val's chair and scratching Cleveland under his chin. "You should've heard the yowling! I thought they were going to *kill* each other!"

"Yeah, but Cleveland beat him up!" said Teddy proudly. "Cleveland's the best fighter on the block. And I fixed him up, Dad," he told Doc. "I wiped off the blood and I put some of that ointment on his nose. You know the stuff you use on me when I skin my knees? Erin didn't help at all," he added. "Blood makes her sick. Boy, are girls dumb! I don't mean

41

you, Vallie," he added quickly. "Just *most* girls."

"Don't forget, Teddy, Erin made a nice warm bed for Cleveland and kept him company until he fell asleep," Mrs. Racer reminded him.

Just then a horn sounded outside.

"That's m'son, Henry, said Mrs. Racer with a smile. She had been the Taylors' housekeeper for ten years, and for ten years her son Henry had picked her up after her day's work, but every night she announced his arrival the same way. It had become a standing joke between the Taylors and her.

"Erin and I made an apple pie, and some applesauce. Teddy and his friends picked so many apples off the tree in the backyard, I hardly knew which way to turn. Erin, where's that bag of apples? I'm going to make apple butter on Monday. Bring you some jars Tuesday. Now Doc, you take it easy, you hear? Teddy, you behave yourself. Erin, heat up that pie so it's nice and warm for Doc and Vallie's dessert. And for goodness sake, don't spend the whole weekend down in the basement practicing that Sugarplum Fairy dance! Get out and play with your friends in the nice fresh air. Vallie, remember you have that science report due on Monday."

She took the bag of apples Erin handed her and glanced at each of her charges. Then she headed reluctantly for the front door, as though during her two-day absence the Taylor household might fall apart.

"Say hi to m'son Henry," called Teddy, trotting after her. Val, clutching warm, furry Cleveland to her chest, giggled.

"Wanna hear the *best* joke?" Teddy asked, after Mrs. Racer had gone.

"Sure. What is it?"

"What's green, covered with warts, and flies faster than a jet?"

Val thought about it for a minute. "I give up. What?"

"Super Pickle! Wanna hear another one?"

Val groaned. "I have a feeling I'm going to hear it whether I want to or not!"

"Then you'll have to hear it while you eat," said Erin, who had put on Mrs. Racer's discarded apron, "or else everything is going to get cold. Wait'll you taste the pie! Mrs. Racer showed me how to make the flakiest piecrust ever."

"And we've got vanilla ice cream, so you can have pie à *la* mud," Teddy put in, trotting beside Doc and Val as they entered the warm, delicious-smelling kitchen.

"That's à *la mode*, dopey!" Erin said with a superior sniff.

"Don't you think I know that?" Teddy said. "I was just tryin' to be funny."

Val caught Doc's eye and grinned, and Doc grinned back as he sat down at the round oak table and spread his blue-and-white checkered napkin on his lap.

"Bring on the food, kitchen wench," he commanded Erin with a comic scowl. "I'm hungry enough to eat a . . ."

Val glared at him.

". . . turnip," he finished.

"One turnip coming right up!" Erin sang out, setting a full plate in front of her father.

Teddy hitched up a chair next to Val. "Okay, here goes — what's purple, more powerful than a locomotive, and leaps tall buildings at a single bound?"

Val woke up early the next morning, her head filled with thoughts of The Ghost. She'd dreamed about him last night — he'd been sailing over jump after jump, each one higher than the last, and she'd been on his back. It was like flying, and in her dream, she heard Teddy's voice saying, ". . . more powerful than a locomotive, able to leap tall buildings at a single bound. . . ." and she'd cried out, "I know — it's Super Ghost!"

"Wrong!" Teddy had said. "It's Super Grape, dummy!"'

Then suddenly a huge jump loomed up ahead. In her dream, Val knew The Ghost could make it. Didn't he have wings, like Pegasus? Only he didn't see it. He couldn't see a thing! The Ghost was blind!

Then he was falling and Val was falling with him, and then he was lying on the ground, his beautiful wings all crumpled and broken. And Cassandra Merrill was standing there, calm and cool, saying, "It wasn't *my* fault. He's just an old, blind horse!"

"That's a very valuable animal," Trevor Merill had told Val accusingly in the dream.

"Valuable. . . ." Cassandra echoed.

What a crazy dream! Val thought. She knew that Doc would go to Animal Inn to check on the horse as soon as he got up, but she couldn't wait till then. She hopped out of bed, dashed into the bathroom to splash cold water on her face and brush her teeth, then hurried back to her room to throw on jeans and a flannel shirt. She brushed her hair and tied it back with a red bandanna, then tiptoed past Doc's, Teddy's, and Erin's doors, and made her way quietly downstairs. There she shushed the dogs who came up to greet her eagerly. Cleveland jumped down from the living room mantel with a solid "plop!" and trotted over to her, making his usual "I'm a poor starving cat who hasn't been fed in so long that I'm about to collapse" noises.

Val let the dogs out to run in the big backyard. She poured some dry cat food into Cleveland's bowl, ignoring the cat's pained expression. Cleveland much preferred canned food to dry.

"If you're really hungry, you'll eat it," she told

45

Cleveland sternly as she rummaged in the vegetable crisper for a handful of carrots. She tossed the carrots and several apples into a plastic bag, let the dogs in, fed them, and hurried out the back door, heading for her bike. She was about to mount and ride off, when she realized that she'd better leave word for the family as to where she'd gone — though she was pretty sure Doc would guess.

She ran back to the house, scribbled a note on the memo board on the refrigerator door, then took off again, the bag of apples and carrots in her knapsack. She wanted to be the very first one to see The Ghost and to learn from Mike how he'd passed the night.

It was usually a fifteen-minute ride to Animal Inn from the Taylors' house, but since it was early on a Sunday morning and there was no traffic on the road, Val made it in close to ten. She hopped off her bike, and propped it against the wall of the Large Animal Clinic. Val dashed inside and headed straight for the stall that housed The Ghost. The horse was standing knee-deep in sweet-smelling yellow straw. Even with the bandage on his right foreleg, he looked comfortable. He pricked up his ears as Val leaned over the door to stroke his velvety nose.

"How're you doing, boy?" she crooned, pressing her cheek to his and drinking in the good, rich horse smell. "I brought you some goodies. How about a carrot?'' She dug into her bag and pulled one out, offering it to him on a flattened palm. The Ghost snuffled at it, then nuzzled her palm delicately as he accepted her gift. While he crunched the carrot, Val stroked his sleek, dappled neck, then scratched behind his gray ears. They looked all soft and fuzzy inside — kind of like pussywillows, Val thought. Everything about him was so *special*! Did Cassandra Merrill know how special he was, and how lucky she was to have a horse like this?

"Oh, Ghost," Val whispered, "I'd give anything to have a horse like you! I'd take such good care of you — I'd brush you ten times a day so your coat would be even shinier than it is now, and as soon as your leg was all better, I'd ride you every chance I got. But I'd never let you work up a sweat — I'd be so careful, and so gentle. And you'd learn to love me as much as I love you!"

The horse made a little whuffling sound, and lightly butted his head against her chest. It was just as though he understood every single word she'd said.

Val took an apple out of the bag and gave it to him with a little sigh.

"But you're *not* mine, so I guess I better try not to get too attached to you. Only I'm afraid it's too late! Maybe I can come and visit you some time after you go back to Longmeadow . . . but you probably wouldn't remember me. I'll remember *you*, though. I'll never, ever forget you as long as I live!"

She flung her arms around The Ghost's neck and hugged him tightly, tears suddenly stinging her eyes.

Glancing up in surprise, Val saw Toby standing there, hands jammed in the hip pockets of his jeans.

"What're you doing here?" she asked, surprised, and a little embarrassed.

"Uh — well, I woke up early and I kept thinking about The Ghost, and I wondered how he was, so I . . . well, I just thought I'd drop in and see," Toby said. He stroked The Ghost's nose. "He looks okay to me."

"His leg's going to be fine," Val assured him. "But there's another problem, one Mr. Merrill didn't know about — " Val didn't want to say anything more.

"What kind of problem?" Toby asked. "Hey, how bad is it? Are you going to cry or something?"

Val blinked rapidly. "No, of course not! But it's pretty bad." She took a deep breath. "The Ghost is going blind. He has cataracts in both eyes. Dad says he'll never jump again."

"Wow, that's bad, all right," said Toby. "What did Mr. Merrill say when Doc told him?"

"He hasn't told him yet," Val said. "He wasn't home when Dad called. I guess he'll be pretty upset. He kept saying how much The Ghost was worth, but if The Ghost can't jump anymore, he won't win any more trophies and prize money. Mr. Merrill will have to put him out to pasture, I guess."

"That's rough," Toby agreed. "But I guess he's earned a nice long rest."

"Want to give him an apple?"

"Yeah, sure." Toby offered the horse one of Val's apples. The Ghost made it disappear in a couple of quick crunches.

"Hey, Val, you got any extras there?" asked Mike, coming out of a smaller stall nearby. Val had been so eager to see The Ghost that she had forgotten Mike would be in the barn taking care of the animals. "I bet ole Sadie here could go for a snack. Eats like a pig, ole Sadie does."

"That's because she *is* a pig!" Val giggled, handing him an apple.

"Well now, that just might be the reason, sure enough," Mike said with a wink. "Here, Sadie." He dropped the apple into the big sow's trough. She gobbled it up with grunts of pleasure.

"What's wrong with her?" Toby asked, peering down at Sadie.

"Some kinda rash," Mike told him. "Don't know m'self what you call it, but Doc knows. Ain't much about animals Doc don't know. Sadie'll be goin' home soon. I been puttin' some ointment on her regular, and looks like all her hair's growin' back. She's Luke

Pollard's prize sow, and he'll be mighty pleased to bring her home, I guess."

He picked up the handles of the wheelbarrow filled with soiled straw and trundled it out of the building, whistling cheerfully.

While Mike and Toby had been discussing Sadie, Val had slipped into The Ghost's stall. Now she was carefully brushing his glossy dappled coat, murmuring soothing words. The Ghost stood quietly, flicking his ears back and forth. Val could tell he was enjoying her gentle touch.

"You're really nuts about that horse, aren't you?" Toby asked, leaning on the door to the stall.

Val nodded. "Yes, I am. I always wanted a horse, and I've helped Doc care for a lot of them, but The Ghost — well, he's special. He's a hero — a champion. I know he'll only be here a few more days, but while he's at Animal Inn, I'm just going to pretend he's mine."

"But he's not," Toby reminded her. "You shouldn't let yourself get too fond of him. It'll only hurt more when he goes back to Longmeadow."

"I know." Val sighed. "But I can't help it."

Toby reached out and scratched The Ghost between his ears. "Yeah, he's a pretty terrific horse, all right. . . ."

"Val! Hey, Val, is that The Ghost? Hey, he's pretty neat! Hi, Ghost. What's up?" It was Teddy, who'd burst into the clinic and dashed right down to The Ghost's stall, closely followed by Erin.

"He's *beautiful*!" Erin breathed. "May I pet him, Vallie? Will it hurt him?"

"No, it won't hurt him," said Val. "Just don't startle him. He doesn't see very well." She smiled at her father. Doc, in sweat pants and T-shirt, entered the stall behind Erin and gave Val a quick hug.

"How's the patient? Looks pretty good to me," he said.

"He's doing fine, Dad," Val told him, then quickly added, "but he won't be able to leave for a while yet, will he? I mean, you'll have to keep a pretty close eye on him, to make sure there's no infection or anything, right?"

"A couple more days, I'd say," said Doc, examining the horse's injured leg, and checking on both scraped knees. "He seems to be in good shape. They'll take excellent care of him at Longmeadow, I'm sure. The Ghost may be old, but he's strong and healthy. He has a lot of good years ahead of him. As you know, Vallie, horses often live to be as old as thirty, sometimes even older. And it's entirely possible that the cataracts can be removed by laser surgery."

"Taylor! Taylor, are you in there?"

Five heads turned in response to the voice that called from the entrance to the Large Animal Clinic.

The two figures in the doorway were only silhouettes against the brightness of the morning outside, but Val immediately recognized Mr. Merrill and Cassandra, and so did Doc and Toby.

"Yes, Mr. Merrill, I'm here," said Doc quietly.

"Got your message last night. Tried to call this morning, but nobody answered. What's the story on my horse? What I need to know is, will The Gray Ghost ever jump again?"

Doc came out of the stall, his expression solemn. "I'm afraid not, Mr. Merrill. Or at least, not until his vision is restored."

"What do you mean, 'his vision'? It's his *leg* I'm concerned about, not his vision! There's nothing wrong with his eyes — is there?"

"I'm afraid there is," said Doc. "Your horse is developing cataracts in both eyes. Things like this happen very gradually, over a period of time. There's a strong possibility that the cataracts can be removed by laser surgery, but not right away. I can put you in touch with an excellent surgeon in Philadelphia, but it will take some time before the condition is operable. In the meantime, the only thing to do is to give the horse the best possible care. And of course he won't be able to enter into competition. Considering his age, I'd advise that you think about retiring him. By all means," Doc added, "have your regular vet check him out, but I'm sure Tom Callahan will say the same thing."

"Daddy, I *told* you The Ghost was too old," Cassandra whined. "He's old and he's going blind! I want a *new* horse. If you don't buy me a new horse, I won't be able to enter the next show!"

"Cassandra, be quiet," said Mr. Merrill sharply. "I'll buy you another horse — I told you I would. And it will be one you can control." He turned to Doc. "If The Ghost is no longer capable of competing, he has no more value to me. Destroy him."

Val felt as if someone had punched her in the stomach.

"*Destroy* him?" she gasped.

Mr. Merrill didn't look at her. His steely eyes were fixed on Doc. "Put him down, if you prefer. But do it immediately. There's no point in prolonging the life of a horse that will never be an asset to Longmeadow Farm. I will, of course, reimburse you for your care of The Ghost up to this point, and for the disposal of his body."

Val was trembling so much she could hardly speak. Clutching her father's arm, she whispered, "Dad, you *can't!*"

Doc lay a reassuring hand over hers. Looking straight at Mr. Merrill, he said, "I'm afraid I'm unable to do that. The Ghost is not my patient — he's Tom

Callahan's. You'll have to speak to Tom about it when he returns."

"Nonsense!" said Mr. Merrill. "I called you in because Callahan was unavailable, and I'm instructing you as to my wishes. I'm a businessman, Taylor. Stocks and bonds are my business. If some of the stocks I invest in turn out to be losers, I sell them. This horse is just another investment as far as I'm concerned. If I could make some money by selling him, I would, but I don't have the time or the patience to look for somebody who would be fool enough to buy The Ghost in this condition. I told you once, now I'll tell you again. Destroy him."

Doc's jaw tightened under his beard. His eyes flashed fire. Very slowly and distinctly he said, "Mr. Merrill, I am a veterinarian dedicated to saving lives. If an animal can't recover from an injury or an illness, I will recommend that it be put out of its misery. But this animal — " he indicated The Ghost with a wave, " — only needs rest and care to restore him to health, though it's possible he'll never again be a champion jumper. I will not put an end to his life. Tom Callahan may agree to do so — I can't speak for him. But as for me, I do indeed refuse."

Val was very proud of her father. He understood how much The Ghost was worth, and it didn't have anything to do with money. She had never hated anyone before in her life, but right then she hated

Mr. Merrill. The Ghost was nothing more to him than a way of making money. But she and Doc knew better.

"You can't just have him killed!" she cried. "It isn't right! It isn't fair!"

"Young lady, you are being insolent," Mr. Merrill growled. "As for you, Dr. Taylor, Callahan returns tomorrow morning. I will contact him immediately, and when he arrives at your — " he looked around contemptuously, " — your Animal Inn, be assured that he will remove The Ghost and carry out my wishes. In the meantime, good day!"

He turned on his heel and stalked the length of the barn, Cassandra trotting at his side.

"Daddy, let's call the Martins just as soon as we get home," Val heard Cassandra say. "I happen to know they're looking for a buyer for Woodhaven's Moonglow. He's a beauty, and he took some firsts at the Devon show last month. And he's young, not all worn out and blind, like The Ghost. . . ." Her voice trailed off as they left the building. A moment later, the engine of their car purred, and its expensive wheels spun on the gravel drive as Mr. Merrill drove away.

Chapter
4

"Never liked that fella, even when he was a little tad. Didn't like his father, either. Come to think of it, his grandpop wasn't nothing to brag about," Mike muttered, as he began forking fresh straw into Sadie's stall.

"Dad, what are we going to do?" cried Val. "We can't just let Dr. Callahan take him away and kill him! It'd be *murder!*"

Doc rubbed his bearded chin and slowly shook his head. "If Tom comes to take him away, there's nothing I can do, Vallie. As I told Merrill, The Ghost is Tom's patient, not mine. And unfortunately, in a situation like this, it's up to the animal's owner. If the owner wants him put down, the veterinarian either does what he's told, or resigns the case — and Longmeadow Farms pays Tom Callahan very well, I imagine, for taking care of their horses."

"For taking *care* of them, not killing them!" Erin put in. "Mr. Merrill is a terrible man! He doesn't care about The Ghost at all. If he doesn't love horses, why does he have so many of them?"

"The Longmeadow horses are an investment — Mr. Merrill keeps them to make money for him. On top of that, I suspect that he likes to see his name in the newspapers as the owner of prize-winning show horses," Doc said. "It makes him feel even more important. Some people need that, Erin. Love has nothing to do with it."

"Dad, you can't let The Ghost be killed! You just can't," cried Val.

"*I* think we oughta kill Cassandra," Toby mumbled.

"Yeah, but if we did, that'd *really* be murder," said Teddy. "And I bet all Mr. Merrill'd do would be to buy a new daughter!"

Val gazed up at her father. "Are you really going to let that awful person decide what happens to The Ghost? Well, if that's the way a vet has to act, maybe I don't want to be one after all!"

She leaned her head against The Ghost's gleaming neck. He was so beautiful — so alive! She wouldn't let him die. She couldn't!

Val felt Doc's hand on her shoulder, but she pulled away from him. If Doc was going to let The Ghost be killed, he was as much the horse's executioner as Dr. Callahan.

57

"Vallie, try to understand. . . ." Doc said softly, but Val refused to meet his eyes.

"I *do* understand!" she whispered. "And I *hate* it! I thought you cared about animals! But if you really did, you wouldn't let The Ghost be murdered! I can't believe *you* would go along with this."

Doc moved away — she could hear his feet in their beat-up sneakers shuffling through the straw.

"Erin — Teddy — time to go home." Doc's voice was low and gentle, "Vallie, we'll talk about this later, okay?"

Val shook her head, unable to speak. Doc had failed her — and The Ghost.

Val stood for a long time, stroking The Ghost's withers, rubbing her cheek against his neck, until she heard Doc's car drive away.

"What're you going to do, Val?"

Toby's voice cut into her thoughts, and at last she raised her head.

"What *can* I do?" she said sadly. "He's going to die. The Ghost is going to die, and we can't do anything about it." Now the tears she'd kept back spilled down her cheeks.

"Maybe we can!" said Toby, coming into the stall. "Listen, Val, I've lived here all my life. I know the country better'n almost anybody. I know places nobody else in Essex has ever even *heard* about!"

"Big deal," Val sighed. "What does that have to do with The Ghost?"

"A lot!" Toby grabbed her arm. "I know this old farm about a mile and a half from here. The house is nothing but a pile of rocks and stuff, but the barn's in pretty good shape. We could hide The Ghost there until they got tired of looking for him!"

"You mean *kidnap* him?" Val gasped.

"Not exactly. Kind of like putting him in protective custody, the way they do on those TV shows. And if nobody knows where he is, we could maybe make a deal with Dr. Callahan or Mr. Merrill. . . ."

"What kind of a deal?" asked Val. "Like hold him for ransom? That's nuts! Mr. Merrill won't want to get him back — he's the one who wants him *killed*, remember? And Dr. Callahan's the hit man! I don't want money, all I want is The Ghost — alive!"

Toby thought about that for a minute. "It might buy him some more time, is all," he said at last.

Val suddenly perked up. "That's it!" she shouted. "That's what we'll do!"

"Okay," said Toby eagerly. "I'll get my oldest brother, Tim, to come over with our cattle truck. We'll put The Ghost in it, and then. . . ."

"No! That's not what I mean!" Val cried. "*Buy* him more time, you said. That's what I'm going to do! I'm going to *buy* The Ghost!"

Toby stared at her. "What're you talking about? You don't have enough money to buy a champion jumper."

"Maybe, but listen!" Val said, her eyes sparkling. "Mr. Merrill and that horrible daughter of his have said The Ghost is worth nothing to them. They'll have to pay Dr. Callahan to put him down, right?"

Toby nodded.

"So what if I offered to buy The Ghost for what it would cost the Merrills to have him destroyed? Or even more? I could promise to pay on an installment plan, the way we got our new refrigerator when the old one pooped out! All Mr. Merrill and Cassandra think about is money. And this way, instead of paying *out* money to get rid of The Ghost, they'd be taking money *in*!"

Toby nodded again. "You might just have something there. You know, Val, for a girl, you've got a lot on the ball."

Val scowled. "Even for a *boy* you have a lot of crazy ideas! But that's okay — it proves you really care about The Ghost."

"Sure, I care!" Toby snapped. "And I care about Doc, too. He's a really good vet, Val. You shouldn't have turned on him the way you did. It's like he said: He couldn't help giving in to what Mr. Merrill said. He didn't have any choice. It wasn't his decision to make."

Val sighed. "I know. Only I just got so upset that he didn't challenge Mr. Merrill to a *duel* or something! And I know, now that I think about it, that he did the best he could for The Ghost. And he *did* stand up to Mr. Moneybags Merrill. But you're right — it wasn't his decision. It's mine, and I've made it, right here and now!"

"So what're you gonna do?" asked Toby.

"I'm going to go to Longmeadow right this minute, and make an offer for The Ghost," said Val, turning to stroke the horse's nose. "And if they don't accept, I'll . . . I'll. . . ."

"You'll what?" Toby asked.

"I'll think of something!"

Breathless from the five-mile bike ride to Longmeadow Farms, Val pressed the doorbell of the Merrill mansion, then pressed it again, impatient to set her plan in motion. Finally, after the third ring, a man appeared who Val supposed was the Merrill's butler. Seeing Val's disheveled appearance, he raised his eyebrows.

"May I help you, Miss?" he asked.

"I hope so!" said Val, brushing a lock of damp hair off her forehead. "Is Mr. Merrill at home? Or Cassandra? I have to see them right away!"

The butler paused, then said, "Mr. and Mrs.

Merrill are out. Miss Cassandra is in the drawing room. May I say who is calling?"

Val nodded vigorously. "Tell Miss Cassandra that Miss Valentine Taylor is here, and if she can't see me right now, I'll just wait until she does!"

Is this really me? Val wondered as soon as the words were out of her mouth. I've never spoken to anybody like this before!

"Er . . . yes, Miss Valentine. Won't you step inside?" offered the butler. "I'll deliver your message to Miss Cassandra."

Val followed him into the spacious entrance hall. For an instant, she had a very strong desire to run, leap onto her bike, and hightail it out of there. But she didn't. She stood, feet firmly planted on the floor, ignoring the frosty gaze of the ladies and gentlemen whose gilt-framed portraits adorned the walls. She wasn't going to let a snooty butler and a lot of pictures scare her away. This was a matter of life and death. She hadn't come all this way to give up now!

The butler returned. "Will you please follow me, Miss Valentine?" he said.

Val followed him into a large, sunny room off the entrance hall. She saw lots of brocaded furniture, more paintings — and Cassandra Merrill on a settee by the fireplace, absorbed in the pages of a magazine. As the butler silently withdrew, a telephone rang, and Cassandra hurried to answer it. Val paused on the threshold, uncertain whether to enter or to tiptoe out after the butler. But the door had silently closed behind him, so she stayed where she was, feeling very uncomfortable. Cassandra's back was turned; she hadn't noticed Val.

"Hello? . . . Oh, hi, Leslie! . . . No, I haven't told my folks yet. I *can't*. After I racked up the last car they gave me, I *can't* tell them I've had another accident with the new one. Especially when I plowed into that car when it stopped at the crossing. . . . I *told* you, I didn't *see* the stop sign! . . . Yes, it's in the shop — not Daddy's regular place, another one. I told him the brakes were acting funny, so I pulled into the nearest service station."

This is none of my business, Val thought. I'll just wait outside. She fumbled with the handle of the door, but it was a strange antique one, not a regular round doorknob, and she couldn't seem to make it work. Leave it to the Merrills to have such a fancy doorknob that I can't open the door, Val thought.

"I guess you wouldn't be willing to lend me the money to pay for the repairs? . . . No, I didn't really think you would. . . . Leslie, I *promised* I'd pay you the fifty dollars I owe you just as soon as I get my next allowance. Can you pick me up tomorrow morning? . . . Thanks, I really appreciate it. Bye."

Cassandra hung up the receiver, turned around, and saw Val.

"How long have *you* been here?" she snapped irritably. "It's not nice to eavesdrop, you know."

"I — I wasn't eavesdropping. Not deliberately, anyway," Val stammered. "The butler showed me in, and then the phone rang, and — well, I couldn't get out. I tried, but I couldn't open the door."

Cassandra flounced back over to the settee and picked up her magazine. "What are you doing here?" Cassandra asked.

Val was suddenly tongue-tied. She felt large, awkward, grubby, and very conscious of the horse smell that clung to her, while Cassandra looked as sleek and well-groomed as one of the models in her magazine. Once again, Val wished she was anywhere else but here, but the thought of The Ghost renewed her courage.

"I . . . I came about The Ghost," she blurted.

Cassandra sighed. "What about him? My father settled everything. I don't see that there's anything more to talk about." She glanced down at the magazine and turned a page, making it very clear that she was much more interested in the new fall fashions than in the fate of an old injured horse.

Val was fighting hard to control her temper, but she managed to keep her voice calm as she said, "Yes, there is. Neither you nor your father have any more use for The Ghost, right?"

"We made that perfectly clear — " Cassandra began, but Val interrupted.

"And you don't care what happens to him so long as he doesn't give Longmeadow Farms any more trouble, right?"

"I wish you'd get to the point," Cassandra said, looking pointedly at the gold watch on her slender wrist. "We're meeting friends of Daddy's and Mother's for lunch and I have to change my clothes."

"Okay, here goes," said Val. "I want to buy The Ghost. I've saved up some money in the bank — I can't get it out today because the bank isn't open, but I can withdraw my savings tomorrow and bring the money after school!"

When Cassandra didn't respond, Val felt her heart sinking into her scuffed boots. She realized how foolish she must sound. This girl had everything money could buy — the sum Val had carefully put away over the past few years seemed like a huge amount to her, but to a girl like Cassandra Merrill it was probably a drop in the bucket. She'll probably laugh in my face, Val thought miserably.

"How much?"

"Wh-what?" asked Val, as Cassandra's question cut through her churning thoughts.

"I said, how much? How much would you be able to pay?" asked Cassandra. Val had her entire attention now, and she wasn't laughing, either.

"Two . . . two hundred dollars," Val faltered. "That's all I have in the bank. But if it's not enough, I get paid for working at Animal Inn, and — "

"Cash?"

"Yes — or I could get a check," said Val breathlessly.

"No, cash would be better." Cassandra nibbled on one polished fingernail, staring intently at Val. "Daddy gave The Ghost to me, you know. He's my horse, so I have the right to sell him if I want to. I *told* Daddy that on the way home this morning, but he said it wasn't worth all the time and trouble it would take to find a buyer. 'Time is money,' he said — he always says that!" It was as though she were talking to herself. Hardly daring to breathe, and trying not to get her hopes up, Val didn't say a word.

"You wouldn't *believe* the expenses I have at Greenbriar — that's the private school I go to outside of Harrisburg. Neither do Daddy and Mother," said Cassandra petulantly. "They give me a piddling little allowance, which is about *half* what the other girls get. Daddy always says if I need more money all I have to do is ask, but sometimes I *can't* ask, know what I mean?"

Val wasn't sure she did, but she nodded anyway.

Cassandra tossed the magazine on the coffee table, and began pacing back and forth across the thick Oriental rug. Val fidgeted, wishing Cassandra would settle down. All that pacing was making her more nervous than she already was.

"Exactly how much of that phone conversation did you hear?" Cassandra asked abruptly, swinging around to face Val.

Startled, Val mumbled, "Everything you said. I didn't mean to, but I kind of couldn't help hearing."

"That's what I thought," said Cassandra, frowning. Then, "Do you *really* want to buy The Ghost?"

"I just *told* you. . . ." Val began.

"Okay, okay. I'll sell him to you for two hundred dollars cash, but on one condition."

"What — what condition?" asked Val.

"You have to promise not to tell my father about my accident with the car, or why I need the money. Because if you *don't* promise, I won't sell." Cassandra smiled unpleasantly. "And if I won't sell, that's the end of The Ghost. And it will all be your fault."

"But that's not fair!" Val said hotly.

"So what?" Cassandra shrugged. "Who said anything about being fair? Well, is it a deal? You pay me two hundred dollars and you don't tell my parents what I'm going to do with it, or else. . . ."

Val swallowed several times. Her mouth was dry. "Deal," she whispered at last. "I'll bring you the money tomorrow after school."

"Super!" Cassandra stood up. "I get home about four. See you then, okay?"

"Okay," said Val. Cassandra accompanied her to the door of the drawing room, and the butler showed her out.

Val got on her bike and pedaled off down the drive that led to the main road. As her shock at Cassandra's heartlessness started to wear off, she began to feel positively giddy with excitement. She was actually going to buy The Ghost! He would be her very own, and then nobody would be able to hurt him again.

It was like the first part of her dream, the good part, when she and The Ghost were flying through the air. She'd saved his life! And maybe she could save his sight as well. The laser surgery Doc had talked about had to be awfully expensive, but she'd start saving up right away. In the meantime, she'd make sure that The Ghost had the very best care in the world. And when his leg was healed, they'd go for rides all over the countryside. Val would be extra careful not to tire him too much, and she'd only ride him on the smoothest roads and trails. She'd be his eyes until he could see again! Oh, how wonderful it was going to be!

Chapter
5

"You're going to buy a horse that's going blind, and your father doesn't even *know*? Val Taylor, you're nuttier than I thought!" Jill Dearborne groaned. Val and her best friend were sitting in Teddy's tree house in the Taylors' backyard, drinking lemonade and eating apples. At least, Jill was eating apples. Val's stomach was tied in knots. She hadn't even been able to eat the big Sunday dinner she'd prepared with Erin's help. In fact, nobody had had much appetite. They'd all been thinking and talking about The Ghost's fate, so Val's silence hadn't caused any comment. Doc, Teddy, and Erin knew how distressed she was. What they *didn't* know was Val's intention to buy the horse from Cassandra Merrill.

Why hadn't she told them? she wondered now, absent-mindedly stroking Cleveland's soft orange fur as the cat lay draped over her lap. But in her heart, Val knew the answer perfectly well. Even though Mr. Merrill was an obnoxious person, it wasn't right to help his equally offensive daughter keep her automobile accident from him. But Val had promised she wouldn't tell anybody, and that included Doc. If her father knew she'd allowed Cassandra to blackmail her into deceiving Mr. Merrill, he might very well forbid her to purchase The Ghost under those conditions. But if she *didn't* buy The Ghost, he'd die! Val hated keeping secrets from Doc, and usually didn't. But this was different. This was a matter of life and death! And she *would* tell him — but not until after The Ghost was bought and paid for. He'd understand . . . wouldn't he?

Val knew she had to talk to somebody, so after Doc had gone out to play pitch-and-catch with Teddy, and Erin had gone into the basement to practice for her Sugarplum Fairy audition, she had called Jill and asked her to come over. She knew she should be working on her science report, but she couldn't concentrate on anything except The Ghost.

As soon as Jill had arrived, they'd scrambled up the ladder to the tree house (Cleveland had shinnied up the trunk), and Val had told her the whole story. Now Jill sat staring at her, her wide eyes seeming bigger than ever. "When are you going to tell Doc? And what do you think he'll say?" she asked.

"Oh, Jill, I don't know!" Putting Cleveland down, Val stretched out on the floor of the tree house, resting her chin on her folded arms and looking down into the yard below. "I guess I have to tell him today — only I don't know how *much* to tell him. He's always said I should save my money for something I really want, and there's nothing in the world I want more than The Ghost. I *can't* let him die, but. . . . Oh, Jill, I know I should have talked to Dad first. It's not exactly like picking up a stray dog or cat. I can't hide The Ghost in my bedroom for a couple of days, the way you did with that kitten you found until you convinced your folks to let you have a pet."

"Not too well," Jill agreed. "Horses eat a lot, too, and I bet horse food's pretty expensive. And it'll be hard work to take care of him. Honest, Val, I don't think Doc's going to be very happy about it."

"I know, you're right," Val sighed. "But the main thing is that The Ghost won't be put down! I'll go to Animal Inn every single day before school to feed him and groom him. And I'll figure out how much his food will cost, and Dad can deduct it from my salary every week. . . ."

"But first, you have to *tell* him," Jill reminded her. "He may not be too happy about it, like you said, but knowing your dad, he'll probably say it's okay. If I were you, I just wouldn't mention your deal with Cassandra. I don't see why he has to know about that. It isn't as if *you'd* done anything wrong."

Val groaned. "That's what I keep telling myself, but somehow I don't believe it." She sat up, wrapping her arms around her knees. "Mom and Dad always taught us that covering up for someone who'd done something wrong was almost as bad as doing it yourself. Maybe I should have gone along with Toby's plan — only that was crazier than what I ended up doing!"

"Who's Toby?" Jill asked. Val realized that in telling the story of The Ghost, she'd never once mentioned Toby. So she filled Jill in, explaining about their bet, Toby's new job at Animal Inn, and finally about his scheme to kidnap The Ghost.

"You're right," Jill agreed. "He's almost as crazy as you! But he sure has some imagination!"

Jill kept Val company for a while longer, but Val was lost in thought and didn't have much to say. Finally Jill announced that she hadn't begun her science report and Val admitted she hadn't, either. They climbed back down to the yard and paid a quick visit to Val's rabbits, Flopsy, Mopsy, Cottontail and Peter, who lived in a pen by the garage, along with Archibald, the duck. Usually snuggling with the bunnies made Val feel good, but this afternoon it didn't work. She couldn't even laugh as Archie waddled around the pen behind brown-and-white Flopsy, though the fact that Archie seemed to think that he was a rabbit himself and Flopsy was his mother almost always made her giggle. Jill headed for home after making Val promise to call as soon as she had spoken to Doc.

Val went up to her room, removed Cleveland from her desk, and tried to force herself to concentrate on the subject of her science report. She had managed to plow through one entry in the encyclopedia when she heard her father and Teddy, accompanied by the dogs, come into the house.

"Vallie? Erin? Where is everybody?" Doc called.

Val called back, "I'm up here, doing my report, and Erin's dancing in the basement. She's been practicing for the Sugarplum Fairy audition all afternoon."

"Dad, can I go over to Billy's for a while?" she heard Teddy ask, and their father answered, "Yes, but be back by five."

"C'mon, Jocko!" Teddy shouted. A moment later the front door slammed behind him.

Val stood up. It was now or never, she decided. She had just reached the door of her room when she heard Doc coming up the stairs. Val came out to meet him, her face solemn, and Doc put his arms around her without a word. She returned the hug fiercely, and murmured, "Dad, I'm sorry I acted the way I did this morning. I was just so upset about The Ghost . . ."

"I know, honey, and so was I. Do you understand why I couldn't play the knight in shining armor and rescue him? I did the best I could under the circumstances."

"Yes, I understand. I still don't think it's fair that an animal's owner has the power of life and death over it, though," said Val. She took her father's hand. "Dad, there's something I have to tell you. . . ." She led him into her bedroom and sat down on the bed. Doc sat beside her.

"What is it, Vallie?" he asked.

"Well. . . ." Val twisted her clenched hands in her lap. "It's true, isn't it, what I just said? About the owner being able to decide if an animal lives or dies?"

Doc nodded.

"Well, suppose the owner who wanted the animal destroyed sold him to somebody who *didn't*?"

Her father looked at her closely. "Val, what are you getting at?"

"I've saved up two hundred dollars, Dad," Val said eagerly. "That's counting birthday and Christmas money from Grandma and Grandpa, and Aunt Ellen and Uncle Jack, and I've put something away every week from my salary. And you said I should wait to spend it until there was something I really wanted. Well, I really want The Ghost! And this morning I offered to buy him, and she said okay!"

" 'She' who? Cassandra Merrill?" Doc asked, frowning.

Val nodded. "That's right. After you and the kids left, I just couldn't stand it anymore, so I biked over to Longmeadow, and Mr. Merrill wasn't in but Cassandra was, so I told her I'd buy The Ghost and I'd pay two hundred dollars cash, and she said she really needed the money. . . ."

"Whoa! Hold on! Wait a minute," said Doc, holding up one hand. "Let me get this straight; Cassandra agreed to sell you The Ghost for two hundred dollars because she needed the money?"

"That's what she said," Val replied, wishing she hadn't mentioned that part of it. "And I promised to pay her tomorrow after school. So you see, The Ghost *doesn't* have to die! I'll take care of him and pay for his board — he can stay in the stall he's in now — you won't even know he's there!"

Doc rose and stood looking down at her, rubbing his beard. He didn't say a single word, and he didn't smile. Val was afraid to know what he was thinking.

"Dad, you're not going to tell me I can't keep him, are you?" she asked in a shaky voice. "I *have* to save him, or else he'll be put to sleep! It's a matter of life and death!"

Doc sat down beside her again and said gently, "Vallie, I have the feeling you're not telling me the whole story, and I think it's time you did." He took Val's chin in one hand and looked into her eyes. "Honey, I understand how you feel about The Ghost and why you want to buy him, but I wish you'd spoken to me about it first instead of rushing off half-cocked. I'm not against the idea — " Val's face lit up " — but something like this can't be entered into lightly. You're laying your life's savings on the line. Also, don't forget that having a horse isn't like having a dog or a cat. Have you thought about how much extra work it will make for Mike, having to take care of The Ghost when you're in school? I know you plan to take care of everything yourself, but it's just not possible. A horse is for keeps, Vallie. And The Ghost may live a very long time. What if you get tired of looking after him? What if — "

"Oh, Dad, I won't! I won't ever! And I wouldn't expect Mike to do everything for him. I'll clean his stall, and exercise him, and — and I'll love him so much! Oh, Dad, please let me keep him!"

Doc sighed. "There's something else to consider. How can you be sure Cassandra will carry out her part of the bargain? You assume The Ghost is hers to sell, but what if he's not?"

"Oh, he is, Dad. She told me so," said Val quickly. "She said Mr. Merrill gave him to her."

"Did you ask to see proof of that?" Doc asked. Val shook her head.

"Then I wouldn't be too sure that Miss Cassandra Merrill is telling the truth, particularly if, as you say, she 'really needs the money.' And that's something else I don't understand — why would a wealthy young lady like Cassandra be so hard up for cash? You don't happen to know, by any chance, do you, Vallie?"

"Well, I . . . that is, she . . . there was this telephone call, and I . . . well, I overheard her telling her friend. . . . Oh, Dad, she had this accident with her car and she needs the money to get it fixed before her parents find out! And she told me that if I told Mr. Merrill, she wouldn't sell me The Ghost and it would be my fault that he'd be killed!"

"Oh, Vallie," said Doc sadly. "Don't you realize that if Cassandra would resort to blackmail, she can't be trusted? Why didn't you tell me all this up front? Don't you trust *me*?"

Val couldn't look at him. "I *do* trust you, Dad. But I was afraid if I told you, you'd tell Mr. Merrill, and then that would be the end of The Ghost!"

Doc put his arm around her and she rested her head on his shoulder. "I . . . wanted to do it all myself," she said. "I didn't . . . think about anything except saving The Ghost." She suddenly pulled away.

"What if he *isn't* really her horse? What if she doesn't even tell Mr. Merrill I offered to buy him, and he goes ahead and tells Dr. Callahan to put The Ghost down? She could do that, couldn't she? And if I hadn't told you what happened, you wouldn't know, and you'd have to let Dr. Callahan take him away, and I'd pay Cassandra the money, and The Ghost would be dead, anyway!"

"Vallie, you're a smart girl," Doc said quietly. "Don't ever let someone else talk you into doing what you feel strongly is not right. If it feels wrong to you, trust yourself."

"Oh, Dad, what a mess!" Val said. "What can we do?"

Doc Taylor stood up. "The first thing is to call Mr. Merrill and speak directly with him. Trevor Merrill is an astute businessman — also a loving, if over-indulgent, father. You know, Val," he said as he headed for the phone in the upstairs hall, "you were not doing either Cassandra or her parents any favors by keeping quiet about her accident. I'd be willing to bet this isn't her first accident — " Val nodded miserably " — and she's lucky it wasn't her last! But if she manages to hide things like this from her parents, she could be responsible for more than a dented sportscar. All life is valuable, Vallie. How many times have you heard me say that? How would you feel if Cassandra Merrill, spoiled brat though she is, were involved in a fatal accident?"

Val whispered, "I didn't think about that. All I was thinking about was The Ghost. I don't like Cassandra, but I wouldn't want to see her hurt."

Doc was dialing now. Val stood beside him, feeling miserable.

"Hello — may I speak to Mr. Merrill? This is Dr. Taylor." There was a pause, then, "Mr. Merrill? It's

78

rather important that my daughter and I see you as soon as possible. . . . Yes, it's about The Ghost. . . . I'd rather not go into it over the phone. Would it be convenient for us to come to Longmeadow around seven this evening? . . . That's right, both of us. . . . No, *not* my other two children and the 'stable boy'! . . . Fine, Mr. Merrill. See you then. Oh, and Mr. Merrill, I think Cassandra should be there, too. . . . Yes, it *is* important. Right. Seven, then. Good-bye."

He hung up the phone and looked at Val. "Well, you heard. We're on for seven. We'll clear this whole thing up once and for all."

"Okay," Val whispered. "I can just imagine what Cassandra's going to do when she hears we're coming over! She'll know I told you, and she'll guess you're going to tell her father about the accident. She's going to be furious!"

"She may be furious, but I for one couldn't care less, and neither should you," said Doc sternly. "If you're going to buy this horse, it has to be without any strings attached, and that means *no secrets*, particularly not from Trevor Merrill."

"What's for dinner? I'm starved!" Teddy shouted as he burst in the front door.

Val shifted her thoughts to what the Taylor family would eat for supper that night. In Mrs. Racer's absence, she was in charge.

"Teddy, please feed the animals *before* you turn on the TV. Then you can help shuck the corn. We'll eat in about half an hour."

Promptly at seven o'clock, Doc and Val were standing at the Merrills' front door, waiting for someone to answer the bell. Val had changed into a plaid skirt and a white blouse; Doc, in honor of the seriousness of the occasion, had put on a shirt, tie, and jacket, and Val thought he looked very business-like and impressive.

When the door finally opened, Val was surprised to see a tall, pretty woman smiling at them. She looked so much like an older version of Cassandra that Val knew immediately that this must be Mrs. Merrill.

"Good evening," said the woman as they entered. "Dr. Taylor and his daughter, am I right?"

"Indeed you are, Mrs. Merrill," said Doc. "My oldest daughter, Valentine."

"Valentine!" Mrs. Merrill repeated. "What a lovely name! Please follow me — our staff has the evening off, I'm afraid, so you must forgive our informality."

Informality! thought Val. Wonder what she'd think if she came to our house!

"My husband and Cassandra are in the drawing room," Mrs. Merrill was saying as her high heels click-clicked across the marble floor.

She walked off down the hall, and Mr. Merrill strode across the room, extending his hand to Doc. "Taylor. Right on the dot, I see."

Cassandra was seated on the very same settee where she'd been earlier that day. Only now her arms were folded tightly across her chest, and she was frowning hard. The look she gave Val would have frozen water in July.

Doc came right to the point. "I understand my daughter has made *your* daughter an offer to buy The Ghost," he said.

"So Cassandra tells me," said Mr. Merrill. "And I also understand that Cassandra has agreed to sell." He was smiling as though that was the best news in the world.

She hasn't told him, Val thought. She's waiting to hear if Doc's going to tell him about the "condition."

Mr. Merrill sank down into a wing chair near the fireplace. "So what's the problem?"

"I just wanted to make sure that Cassandra had the right to sell The Ghost to Vallie," said Doc. "I'm agreeable to the transaction, but I want to be perfectly certain that The Ghost is hers to sell."

Mr. Merrill glanced at Cassandra, who didn't meet his eyes. "Well, Taylor, I can see that you're a very astute businessman. Actually, The Ghost belongs to me. It's true I gave him to Cassandra, but on paper, he is still my property."

"That's what I figured," said Doc. "Are you willing for Vallie to purchase your horse for two hundred dollars? He's worth a lot more than that."

Dad! Val cried inwardly.

"He *was*," said Mr. Merrill. "At the moment, considering his infirmity, he's worth very little. If my daughter has made a deal for two hundred dollars, I'd say it's a fair figure."

Again Doc looked over at Cassandra, but she refused to speak. "I am willing to allow Vallie to buy the horse, provided you understand the terms of the 'deal,' as you call it," he said.

"Terms? What terms?" asked Mr. Merrill, raising his eyebrows.

Doc gazed straight at Cassandra as he spoke. "Cassandra is willing to sell The Ghost to Vallie on the condition that Vallie not tell you about an accident she had with her car. She intended to use the money for repairs."

As Val watched, she saw Cassandra's expression change from sullen calm to rage. But if Val had expected Cassandra to be ashamed because her secret had been revealed, she was very much mistaken. Instead, Cassandra suddenly smiled.

"Dr. Taylor is absolutely right, Daddy," she said. "I *did* have another accident, and I didn't want to worry you or Mother, so I didn't tell you. After all, it wasn't my fault."

Where have I heard that before? Val thought to herself.

"I thought that the smart thing to do was to figure out what *you'd* do if something like this happened to *you*," Cassandra continued calmly, "and I decided to make a deal, just the way you would. That's when I got in touch with Val and offered to sell The Ghost — "

Val felt her mouth open in astonishment. She quickly closed it.

" — and like I said before, I didn't want to upset you and Mother, so I planned on having the car fixed so you'd never know. I mean, otherwise I bet you'd have gotten mad and *sued* that poor guy who ran into me, and that would've cost an awful lot of money."

Val and Doc looked at each other. Val wanted to say something, but the look in her father's eye warned her to let Mr. Merrill speak first.

"Cassandra," he said proudly, "you're a chip off the old block! You're right — that's exactly what I would have done in similar circumstances." He turned to Doc, beaming. "If there's one thing Cassandra understands, it's the value of money. I'll be more than happy to make out a bill of sale for The Ghost — but since Cassandra made the deal, I guess in all fairness I'll have to turn the money over to her.

Cassandra, honey," he said to his daughter, "I'll have my mechanic pick up your car first thing tomorrow morning. Benny can fix it up as good as new, and I'll foot the bill."

"Oh, Daddy, I knew you'd understand!" cried Cassandra, jumping up from the settee and running to throw her arms around her father. "You're the best daddy in the whole wide world!"

Val and Doc were silent during the first part of the drive home. Both were stunned by the way Cassandra had managed to manipulate the situation — and her father.

"I just can't *believe* it!" Val burst out at last. "It was a pack of lies — every single thing she said! The other car didn't run into her, she ran into him! and she didn't contact me, *I* contacted *her*!"

Doc shook his head. "I'm afraid that young lady wouldn't know the truth if it bit her in the leg. But sooner or later she's going to trip herself up. Lies have a way of catching up to the liar."

After another brief silence, Val said, "People have funny ways of showing that they love somebody, don't they? I mean, *your* way is so different from Mr. Merrill's way. And Cassandra — well, I don't think she loves anybody as much as she loves herself!"

Doc reached over and squeezed her hand. "For a kid who's hardly dry behind the ears, you're not too dumb," he teased.

Val grinned. "I have a pretty good teacher — guess I'm just a 'chip off the old block'!"

Chapter
6

When Doc and Val got home, Teddy was watching TV, and Erin was in the basement practicing for her audition. Val called to her to come up and hear some good news, and as she listened Erin continued to practice leaps and turns around the living room. When she heard that Val was really going to keep The Ghost, she leaped so high her hands nearly brushed the ceiling. When Erin and Teddy had finally calmed down, Val helped them get ready for bed.

"You mean you're really going to buy The Ghost? Honest and truly?" Teddy spluttered through a mouthful of toothpaste bubbles. "Can I ride him? Can I help you take care of him?"

"I think Cassandra Merrill is just about the most awful person I have ever heard of in my entire *life*," said Erin. "She doesn't deserve to have a beautiful horse like The Ghost!"

"Well, she doesn't anymore," said Val happily. "Mr. Merrill wrote out a bill of sale, and Dad's meeting me tomorrow at lunchtime to take me to the bank.

He'll hang onto the money until he picks me up after school, and then we're going to Mr. Merrill's office to pay him."

"Wow!" Teddy shouted, diving into his bed. "A horse! We've got a *horse*!"

"*Val's* got a horse," Erin corrected. "She's spent every cent she had in the world! Oh, Val," she cried, throwing her arms around her sister's waist, "I'm so happy for you! Aren't we lucky? You've got the thing you wanted most, and I'm going to be the Sugarplum Fairy in *The Nutcracker*!"

"And I've got a *sister* who has a horse! Boy, wait'll I tell Eric and Billy! All Eric has is gerbils, and Billy only has his dumb old dog!"

Doc had come upstairs to say good night to the younger children, and now he laughed. "Well, until today, *we* only had *two* dumb old dogs — and Cleveland, and a canary and the rabbits and Archie, and your hamsters," he told Teddy. He glanced over at the Habitrail on Teddy's bureau. "You'd better take them into my study. You know they keep you awake, running all night in their wheel."

Teddy groaned and hopped out of bed, picking up the Habitrail and trotting with it out the door. "It's only Paula who runs all the time. John, George, and Ringo just chew on things."

When he came back, Doc tucked him in and gave him a good-night kiss, then went into Erin's room. She was sitting up in bed, a book of ballet photographs on her knees.

"Turn out your light at nine, Erin, okay?" he said. "And Erin. . . ."

"Hmm?" Erin reluctantly tore her eyes away from a picture of Cynthia Gregory to look up at her father.

"Honey, you're *auditioning* for the Sugarplum Fairy, and so are a lot of other girls. I know you're a good dancer, but you're only eleven. It's entirely possible that Miss Tamara may decide to give the part to an older girl, one with more experience," Doc said gently, stroking Erin's hair. "Don't set your heart on winning the role, because you may be in for a big disappointment."

But Erin shook her head. "No, Daddy. I'm absolutely *sure* I'll get it. I know every single step! I'm going to practice every minute I can before next Saturday, too. Mrs. Racer will make my costume — she promised she would. A pink tutu, with a sparkly bodice, just like the one Mommy wore. I gave her a picture and she's sure she can copy it. Oh, Daddy, Vallie's dream came true — now it's my turn!"

Val had come in to say good-night to her little sister, and said, "If anyone deserves to get the part, it's you, Erin. I'll be keeping my fingers crossed all week!"

"In that case, you'd better finish that science report right away," said Doc with a grin. "It's pretty hard to type with your fingers crossed."

"Oh, Daddy!" Erin giggled. "You're silly!"

" 'Night, Erin. 'Night, Dad," said Val. As she left Erin's room, she added, "Maybe I'll just have to learn to type with my toes!"

If Val had had trouble concentrating on her science report earlier that afternoon, it was nearly impossible now that she knew The Ghost would definitely be hers. *Her* horse! Her very own horse! She could hardly wait to tell Jill in the morning. And Toby — wait till he heard! Suddenly Val just couldn't wait to tell him that she was going to buy The Ghost. She dashed out into the hall and picked up the phone, then realized she didn't know his number. After a quick check in the phone book, she dialed, waiting impatiently for somebody to answer.

"Currans'," said a deep voice at last. It wasn't Toby's, Val knew.

"Hello — this is Val Taylor. Can I speak to Toby?" she asked.

"Sure. Just a minute."

Val heard the deep voice yell, "Hey, Toby, it's some girl."

"Hello?" *That* was Toby's voice.

"Toby it's me, Val. Guess what! The Merrills are going to sell me The Ghost! It's all going to be okay! He won't have to die!"

"Hey, Val, that's great! I never thought you'd

be able to do it. Congratulations! Uh . . . Val, do you think maybe I could ride him some time . . . when his leg's better, I mean?"

Val paused. Let someone else ride her very own horse? Well, why not? Maybe she'd let him ride The Ghost once in a while as long as Toby was very, very careful. "Sure. I'll let you ride him. Only not until he's completely recovered."

"Fantastic! Thanks for calling, Val. I really mean it. I've been thinking about that horse ever since you told me you were going to try to buy him. I thought it was a really nutty idea, but I'm glad it worked out. The Ghost is something special, you know?"

"Yes, I know," said Val softly. "See you later, okay?"

"Okay! Bye!"

Val hung up and wandered back to her room, smiling. Maybe she'd let Teddy ride The Ghost too, but only when she was leading him around the field behind the barn. If Erin wanted to take a turn, that would be all right, too. But Erin wasn't much of a horse person. She probably loved The Ghost because he was beautiful and graceful, like a ballet dancer.

It was close to ten o'clock when Val finally finished typing the final draft of her report. She knew it wasn't the best work she'd ever done, but at least it was finished. Her shoulders ached and her eyes were watery.

Her last thought, after she'd fallen into bed and right before she fell asleep, was, Tomorrow it'll all come true. Erin was right — my dream is coming true!

"What if Mr. Merrill changes his mind?" asked Teddy the next morning as he dug into his bowl of raisin bran cereal. "What if he decides he doesn't want to sell you The Ghost after all?"

"He can't!" Val said at once. "He won't — will he, Dad?"

Doc, who was fixing himself some cinnamon toast, shook his head. "It's extremely unlikely. Mr. Merrill may be a lot of things, but he's not a welsher."

"What's a welsher, Daddy?" asked Erin.

"A welsher is somebody who breaks an agreement and goes back on his word," said Doc. "If Mr. Merrill, after writing out a bill of sale for the horse, decided he didn't want to sell after all, I'm sure he knows that all of Essex would hear about it. Now, if Vallie had gone ahead and made a deal with Cassandra, that would be another story."

"Cassandra," said Teddy, scowling, "is the *pits*!"

Val very definitely agreed. Nevertheless, she couldn't help feeling worried as she walked to the corner where the bus picked her up for Alexander Hamilton Junior High. It would be almost four hours before she could take her money out of the bank, and three hours more before she would turn over her savings to Mr. Merrill. So much could happen in that time!

But it didn't. At half past three, Val and Doc were ushered into Mr. Merrill's office in downtown Essex, and Val proudly handed him a fat envelope containing twenty crisp new ten-dollar bills. The teller at the Farmers and Mechanics Bank and Trust had asked her how she wanted the money, and Val had decided on tens rather than two one-hundred dollar bills. It looked like more, somehow, even though the value was the same. Her bank account now had only seventeen dollars and forty cents, but that was all right. She'd start saving again right away to pay for The Ghost's operation. Plus, she didn't have a saddle or bridle for him yet, but she'd worry about that later. The most important thing was to save him from the Merrills.

"You can count it if you like" said Val quickly, "but I'm sure it's all there. The teller counted it twice."

"That won't be necessary," said Mr. Merrill. He looked at the envelope in his hand, then glanced up at Doc. "I hope you realize you've made a very good deal here, Taylor. If I'd been willing to invest some time, I could probably have gotten a lot more for The Ghost, even in his present condition."

"Mr. Merrill, I don't think you understand the situation," said Doc quietly. "*I* didn't make the deal, and neither did Cassandra. Vallie did. You're holding in your hand my daughter's entire savings. . . ."

"Except for seventeen dollars and forty cents," Val put in.

"Except for seventeen dollars and forty cents," said Doc. "Vallie has been saving a little bit of every paycheck. It's her money, and she's earned the right to spend it on something she considers very important. The Ghost is that important to her."

Mr. Merrill's gaze turned from Doc to Val. Val saw an expression of uncertainty and surprise on his face. "This is *your* money?" he asked.

Val nodded. "But I didn't really earn it all. Some of it was from Christmas and birthday presents from my aunts and uncles and my grandparents. . . ."

"Never mind that," said Mr. Merrill impatiently. "The fact is that you've used it to buy The Ghost. Why?"

"Why?" Val echoed. It was a silly question. "Because I love him. I've loved him for years, ever since my parents started taking me to horse shows and I saw him jump. I just couldn't let him die!" Val was surprised to see that Mr. Merrill's expression was still puzzled. "Don't you understand?" she asked.

Mr. Merrill smiled then, and it was a *real* smile. "I think I'm beginning to," he said. He looked at Doc. "Dr. Taylor, you're a very lucky man."

"I think so," said Doc.

There was a long pause; then Mr. Merrill pushed the button of the intercom on his desk and said, "Ms. Howard, please make out a receipt to Miss Valentine Taylor for two hundred dollars. The young lady will pick it up on her way out."

"Thank you for your time, Mr. Merrill," said Doc, and the two men shook hands.

"Not so fast," Mr. Merrill said sharply, and Val cringed inside. Was something wrong?

"There's an item that hasn't been considered," said Mr. Merrill, "and that's The Ghost's tack. I don't imagine you have any of the necessary pieces of equipment for a horse, do you?"

"Well, no," Val faltered. "But I won't be able to ride him for a while, and. . . ."

"That's all taken care of," Mr. Merrill barked. "Sean will deliver The Ghost's saddle and bridle, along with several halters and blankets to Animal Inn this afternoon. It's included in the purchase price — something I neglected to mention last night."

A big smile spread over Val's face. She looked at her father.

"That's very kind of you," Doc said quietly. "I'm sure Vallie appreciates your generosity."

"Oh, I do!" cried Val. "Thank you!"

"That's settled, then," said Mr. Merrill. He turned to Val, stretching out his hand. She took it and clasped it warmly.

"You can come and see The Ghost any time — if you want to, that is," she said.

"Thank you, Valentine. Good luck with The Ghost. He's a fine animal. I'm glad he's found a — a loving home."

Mr. Merrill sat down in his big leather chair and began going through his papers again.

Doc put his arm around her shoulders, and they headed for the door. Mr. Merrill's secretary handed Val a neatly typewritten receipt. Val stared at it for a long time, then whispered to Doc, "It's really *real*! He's mine now! The Ghost is *mine*!"

"He sure is," said Doc. "And I have a great idea. How about going out to Animal Inn and telling him all about it?"

Val grinned. Doc understood her better than anyone in the world!

"I think that's absolutely the best idea I've ever heard!" she said.

Together, they hurried out of Mr. Merrill's office to Doc's car — and to The Ghost!

Chapter
7

"Val, that's fantastic!" cried Sarah Jones. Sarah played shortstop for the Hamilton Raiders, the girls' softball team on which Val played first base. Val was sitting with a tableful of eighth-grade girls in the Alexander Hamilton cafeteria the following day, and she'd just told everyone about her purchase of The Ghost. She still couldn't quite believe it herself — but telling her friends made it seem more real.

"And she bought him with her very own money," Jill added.

"He's a champion, isn't he?" asked Lisa Ahrens. "I used to read about Longmeadow's Gray Ghost in the papers. Are you going to ride him at Madison Square Garden? Boy, you'll be *famous*!"

"No, I'm afraid not," said Val, taking a bite of her taco. "The Ghost won't ever jump again. He's fifteen years old, and he can't see very well. But when his leg is better, Dad says he'll make a fine saddle horse, and there's a vet he knows in Philadelphia who might be able to fix his eyes. Besides, The Ghost's famous enough already. He doesn't need to win any more prizes."

Lila Bascombe, who was not one of Val's best friends, finished her hamburger. She wiped her fingers on a paper napkin, and said, "I don't see what's so great about buying an old, blind horse with a bad leg. If *I* was buying a horse, I'd want one that was in good condition."

Val smiled sweetly at Lila. "Buying a horse isn't like buying a car, Lila. A horse is *alive*. And *this* horse is something special. He's — he's . . ." She struggled to find the right words, "he's a member of our family now. If my *sister* hurt her leg and was going blind, I wouldn't trade *her* in for a new model!"

Everyone giggled, and Lila flushed. "What I meant was, I don't think you got much for your money. My dad says you have to be smart to make good investments, and my dad is *very* successful."

She sounds like Cassandra Merrill, Val thought. Lila's opinion wasn't very important to Val.

"My dad's successful, too," Val retorted. "He may not make a lot of money, but he saves lives — animals' lives. And like he always says, all life is valuable. If it wasn't for him, The Ghost would've been killed!"

"Well, if you're happy with an old beat-up horse that nobody else wants, that's fine with me," said Lila, picking up her tray and standing up. She'd seen

Andy Winston heading her way. Andy was tall and nice-looking; plus he was the president of the ninth grade. Lila's eyes suddenly began to glitter. They reminded Val of the look Cleveland got before he tried to pounce on a bird. Val felt sorry for Andy Winston.

Val dumped her paper plate and napkin into a container by the door, and started off with Jill for her afternoon classes. No matter what Lila Bascombe said, she knew in her heart that The Ghost would always be a winner!

"Hey, Val, wake up," said Jill, grabbing Val's arm. "You almost walked right past the bio lab!" Jill shuddered delicately. "I *hate* bio! If we have to cut up another frog, I'm going to throw up. I'm awful glad you're my partner — you always know just what to do."

The girls hurried to their seats. "I have to be good at things like that," said Val matter-of-factly. "You know I'm going to be a vet, like my dad. And dissection is the best way to learn how an animal's body works."

"You know, Val, you're strange," said Jill. "You won't eat meat 'cause you love animals so much, but you can slice right into that poor little frog. I bet if you went to a fancy French restaurant and there were frogs' legs on the menu, you wouldn't eat them."

"You bet I wouldn't!" Val replied. "But it's different when it's in a lab. There's a *reason* for it, not just feeding your face. By learning about animals, I can help them when I grow up."

"If Val Taylor and Jill Dearborne will kindly give me their attention, class can begin," said Ms. Lessing, the science teacher. Val and Jill both flushed, and focused their attention on Ms. Lessing. But Val's mind immediately wandered. How was The Ghost feeling today? Would he be glad to see her when she came to visit him after school? Did he know he belonged to her now, and not to that awful Cassandra and Mr. Merrill?

But maybe Mr. Merrill wasn't so awful after all. When she and Doc had gone to see the horse after leaving his office, one of Longmeadow's station wagons had pulled up next to the barn. Sean had delivered a saddle, two bridles, a halter and lead line, and two beautiful green blankets trimmed with white. Val had immediately taken over one of the unoccupied stalls as The Ghost's tack room, and Mike had promised to construct proper racks for all the equipment. Maybe tomorrow, after the clinic was closed, Doc would let her start working on fixing it up. She knew exactly what she wanted to do — she'd sweep out the stall, and put down some of the leftover linoleum from the kitchen at home. And then she'd make frames for the pictures of The Ghost she'd cut out of the papers, and hang them on the walls. And then. . . .

"Val!" Jill poked her in the ribs, and Val blinked. "Ms. Lessing just asked you a question!" Jill hissed.

"What was it?" Val hissed back.

"She asked you to describe the circulatory system of the leopard frog," Jill whispered. "And if you don't answer real quick, she'll ask *me*, and I don't remember a single thing!"

"Uh . . . the leopard frog has blood that's a lot like humans, only its heart has three chambers instead of four. . . ." Val began. She managed to muddle through somehow, but when the class was over, the teacher asked her to stay behind for a few minutes.

"Val, dear, you've always been one of my best students," said Ms. Lessing, after the other kids had left, "and I know you plan on becoming a veterinarian. But for the past two days, you've been on Cloud Nine."

"Uh . . . I'm sorry, Ms. Lessing," Val said, blushing. Science was her best subject and Ms. Lessing was one of her favorite teachers. She hated to let her down. "I guess I've had — other things on my mind."

"Like what, for instance?" the teacher asked.

So Val told her all about The Ghost. When she had finished, Ms. Lessing said, "I can understand

100

why you're so excited, but suppose you try to get your mind back on your work, at least during class. You can think about your horse *after* school."

Val nodded. "I'll try. I really will." She glanced at the clock on the wall. "Golly, I'd better get moving! if I'm late for English, Mr. Steele will kill me!"

Ms. Lessing smiled. "I doubt that. But run along, Val. If Mr. Steele wants to know why you're late, tell him I kept you after class. And congratulations on The Ghost. Maybe one day I'll drop by Animal Inn and you can introduce us."

"Oh, would you? That'd be wonderful! Any time — any time at all. . . . I'm coming, Jill," Val told her friend who had been waiting, more or less patiently, by the classroom door.

"I was just telling Ms. Lessing about The Ghost," she said as they dashed down the hall.

"I know — I heard," Jill puffed. "Even if I hadn't heard, I could have guessed. It's all you ever talk about these days!"

"I can't help it," said Val happily. "I just can't seem to think about anything else. Hey, want to come out with me to see him after school?"

"Can't," Jill said. "Chorus practice. And you've got softball practice, remember."

"I know, but maybe I can leave early. I haven't seen him since yesterday afternoon!"

"Maybe you ought to ask Doc to put a phone

in The Ghost's stall," Jill teased. "Then you could call him up and talk to him during the day."

Val giggled, then frowned when she saw that the door to their English class was closed. "Rats! We *are* late! Hope we haven't missed anything."

They tiptoed guiltily to their seats as Mr. Steele was saying, "The next book report will be due in three weeks. Anybody ready to tell me what book he or she will be reading?"

Val's hand shot up, along with several others.

"Yes, Valentine?"

"*National Velvet*," said Val. "I've already started it. It's a wonderful book, about a girl who gets this wonderful horse. . . ."

Jill groaned.

"Vallie, I think you ought to talk to Doc," said Mrs. Racer when Val came home that afternoon after softball practice.

"Why? What's wrong?" Val asked.

"It's Erin. She's got a nasty sore throat, but she won't stop practicing her dancing. I finally got her to drink some nice hot tea with lemon and honey and made her lie down for a while, but she says she's going to get right up again and go over some steps. Maybe Doc can do something with her."

"Does she have a fever?" Val asked, as she picked up Cleveland and gave the big orange cat a hug.

Cleveland purred noisily, and rubbed his head against Val's chin.

"She won't let me put a thermometer in her mouth," Mrs. Racer sighed. "But she's all red in the face, and I don't like the look of her."

With Cleveland slung over her shoulder, and Jocko and Sunshine trotting at her heels, Val bounded up the stairs and into Erin's room. She found her sister lying on the bed, her favorite book of ballet photographs open on her stomach and "The Nutcracker Suite" playing on her stereo. Dandelion, Erin's canary, was singing along.

"Hi, Erin. How're you feeling?" she asked, sitting on the edge of the bed. Cleveland leaped out of her arms and crouched at the foot of the bed, narrowed yellow eyes fixed on the canary, tail lashing. Jock and Sunshine rested their chins on the mattress and looked at Erin.

"Oh, I'm okay," said Erin brightly. "But I told Mrs. Racer my throat was scratchy, and she acts like I have the plague or something."

Val touched Erin's forehead. It was warm, but not burning.

"You better stay in bed, like Mrs. Racer told you," she said. "I'll ask her to bring up some hot soup a little later. But for now, you rest. You don't want to be sick for your audition Saturday."

"I won't be!" said Erin. "Lots of kids in my class

have colds. I'll be okay in the morning." She grabbed Val's hand. "And Vallie, please don't tell Daddy I'm not feeling good. I don't need to go to the doctor. Honest, tomorrow I'll be just fine."

"I can't not tell Dad," said Val, "and even if I didn't, Mrs. Racer would. Now you stay right where you are, okay? I'm going to Animal Inn for a while, just to check on The Ghost. While I'm gone, don't you dare dance a *step*!" she added, knowing she sounded bossy, but also knowing that when Erin set her mind on something, the only way to prevent her from doing it was to be very, very firm.

"But there's one section in the Sugarplum Fairy's solo that I have to work on," Erin insisted. "I have to be *perfect* on Saturday! And I only have three more days!"

Val glanced at her wristwatch. Time was slipping away so fast, precious time that she could be spending with The Ghost. "Erin, if you don't promise me you'll rest till Dad and I get home, I'm going to call him right now, and he'll tell you the exact same thing!" she said sharply. "If you get all hot and sweaty and overtired, then you'll *really* be sick. I'm going now — be back around six."

As Val scooped up Cleveland and dashed out the door, she heard Erin grumbling, "Val, you're mean and bossy, that's what you are!"

Val hurried into the kitchen, where Mrs. Racer

was stirring a big pot of her famous chicken-corn soup. "She'll stay put, I think," Val told her, grabbing some apples. "I'm going to Animal Inn — I'll come home when Doc does. Mmmm — that soup smells delicious!"

Tossing the apples into her knapsack, Val ran outside and hopped on her bike. She was halfway down the street when she heard Teddy's voice shouting, "Hey, Val, wait up!"

Reluctantly, Val braked. A moment later, Teddy came pedaling up next to her.

"Teddy, I'm in a hurry! What do you want?" she asked.

"I'm comin' with you," said Teddy, beaming. "I haven't seen The Ghost yet."

Val sighed. "Yes, you have, Teddy. You saw him on Sunday."

"Yeah, but that was when he belonged to those Merrills. I haven't seen him since you bought him. C'mon, let's go! And Billy and Eric want to come, too — they're waiting at Billy's house."

It was all Val could do not to yell, "Teddy, go home!" It would take forever to ride to Animal Inn with Teddy and his friends, since they weren't allowed to take their bikes on the main roads. That meant she'd have to go down all the side streets. By the time she got to The Ghost, it would be just about time to turn around and go home for supper!

She scowled at her brother. "Teddy . . ." she began, then the look on his face stopped her short. Sometimes being the oldest was awfully hard. . . . "Okay, come on then," she said. "But you and Eric and Billy stay right behind me, single file, and stop when I stop and go when I go. And *no racing!*"

Val led the little procession slowly and carefully along the tree-lined streets of suburban Essex until, what seemed like hours later, they reached Animal Inn. There were only a few cars in the parking lot in front of the Small Animal Clinic — Doc's and two others. As Val and her crew pedaled down the gravel path that led to the barn, she sniffed one of her very favorite smells: fresh-cut grass. She noticed that the lawn had been mowed, and a moment later Toby appeared around the corner of the barn, riding Doc's power mower.

"Hi, Val," he called over the roar of the engine. "Guess what? Harvey had six babies this morning! And they don't have any hair! Hey, Teddy, how ya doing?"

Teddy leaped off his bike. "Can I run the mower?" he asked eagerly. "Dad lets me sometimes."

"Aw, come on, Teddy," said Eric. "We wanna see your sister's horse!"

"Yeah — where is he? Is he in there?" asked Billy, pointing at the Large Animal Clinic.

"Sure is. Come on, Billy, Eric," Val said, leading

the way. "But you must be quiet, and no running around, because there are some sick animals in here, too, and we shouldn't disturb them."

"What's in the knapsack, Val?" Eric asked.

"Apples for The Ghost," Val told him.

"Can I give him one?" asked Billy hopefully.

"Me, too!" cried Eric.

"Sure, you both can. But first, let's say hello to my horse," said Val.

As they entered the barn, Val wondered if The Ghost would really remember her. It seemed as though he did. His ears pricked forward, and he nuzzled her neck, whuffling softly in her ear. Then he stretched out his neck and sniffed over her shoulder — the apples! He smelled the apples!

"Oh, Ghost," Val sighed, putting her arms around his neck and giving him a hug. "I thought it was *me* you were so glad to see!" But she couldn't help grinning. She took off the knapsack, then took out an apple and offered it to him on the flat palm of her hand. He accepted the treat daintily and crunched while Val stroked him.

"Boy, is he *big*!" said Billy, peering over the stall door. "You'd need a ladder to get up on him!"

"Can we pat him?" asked Eric. "Does he bite?"

"Sure, you can pat him, and no, he doesn't bite *people*, only apples," Val told him.

"He doesn't *look* blind," Billy said.

"He isn't, not completely," said Teddy. "Isn't he a great horse?" he asked his pals.

"Is he really famous?" Billy asked Val. "Teddy says he has won lots of prizes."

"He's famous, all right," said Val, smiling. "But I'd love him even if he wasn't."

"Hey, Val, I just got a great idea," said Toby, coming over to give The Ghost a pat. "Remember how at Longmeadow they had a fancy sign on his door with his name on it? Well, I could make one in wood shop at school. I've been saving a real nice piece of cherry wood for something special — how about this? 'Val Taylor's Gray Ghost'?"

"Oh, Toby, that would be wonderful!" Val cried. Then she thought a minute and added, "But the old sign didn't say 'Trevor Merrill's Gray Ghost.' It said 'Longmeadow's Gray Ghost'. . . ."

"Then how about 'Animal Inn's Gray Ghost'?" Toby suggested.

"That's perfect!" Val's eyes shone with excitement. "And maybe you could make some frames for the pictures I have of him. I want to hang them in the tack room. I have it all planned out in my head. Come on — I'll show you what I'm going to do."

While Val explained to Toby how she was going to fix up the empty stall, Teddy, Billy, and Eric admired The Ghost for a while longer. Then Teddy showed his friends the other animals in the barn — Sadie the sow, Mr. Henderson's cow Daisy with the infected hoof, and Scruffy, a goat with indigestion. Val showed Eric and Billy how to give the horse an apple — hand stretched out flat, so the fingers didn't get bitten by mistake — and after a lot more loving pats and gentle words in The Ghost's ear, Val reluctantly left him, promising to see him the next afternoon.

"See you tomorrow, I guess," said Toby, as he mounted his bike. "Doc says I can go along when he takes a look at Mr. Morgan's sick calf, since I know a lot about cows," he added proudly. "And then he wants me to wash the van, and do some other stuff around here."

"Okay — see you then," said Val. "C'mon guys, time to go!"

Toby took off at top speed down Orchard Lane, and Val, Teddy and his friends swung by the Small Animal Clinic to wave and say hi to Doc, who was just locking up.

"Meet you back at the house," he called, heading for his car. Val began leading her little group along Butternut Road. In her mind, she could just see the cherry wood plaque Toby was going to make, all polished and shiny, hanging on the door of The Ghost's stall. She decided that Toby wasn't as much of a pain as she'd thought at first. In fact, he was pretty nice when you got to know him. And he really cared about The Ghost. . . .

"Val, what's the matter with you?" Teddy shouted. Val looked back over her shoulder, to see Teddy, Billy, and Eric pausing at a stop sign she'd just sailed past. "You coulda gotten *killed*!" he added, carefully looking both ways before he pedaled ahead.

"You're right," Val said. "I wasn't paying attention. Why don't you be a leader, Teddy, at least for the next few blocks?"

Teddy's face lit up. "Okay! I'll be real careful, just you watch." As he passed her, Val heard him say to Eric and Billy, "Ever since she bought The Ghost, my sister's been all *ferdutzed*!"

Val couldn't help laughing. *Ferdutzed* was one of Mrs. Racer's Pennsylvania Dutch words. Like *ferhoodled*, it meant all mixed up, not thinking straight. And I guess I am, she thought. I'm *ferhoodled* and *ferdutzed*, all right!

Chapter 8

The next two days flew by. Erin's sore throat seemed to have magically disappeared. She still had a slight case of the sniffles, but it wasn't enough to keep her home from school, or from practicing for her audition on Saturday. After school on Thursday, Val zipped out to visit The Ghost for a while, and came home to find Mrs. Racer looking worried.

"Erin's got spots," Mrs. Racer told Val and Doc. "She kept scratching her tummy, and I made her let me look. Seems like chicken pox to me. I remember when m'son Henry had 'em — you, too, Vallie. They always come out on the tummy first."

"Four kids in my class have chicken pox," Teddy put in cheerfully. "And they can't go to school for a whole week! They have to be *caroteened*!"

"That's *quarantined*, Teddy," said Doc. He turned to Erin. "Erin, show me your stomach."

"Oh, Daddy, it's not chicken pox, I know it's not!" cried Erin, dodging away. "I bet it's an allergy. I bet I'm allergic to — to *Cleveland*!"

Cleveland who had been sitting on the kitchen table, gave her a dirty look, jumped down and stalked off, tail in the air.

"Erin, let me look," said Doc firmly. "Just lift up your shirt a little so I can see your tummy."

Teddy suddenly spoke up, eyes sparkling. "If she does have chicken pox, can I touch her? 'Cause then I can be *caroteened* too! Come on, Erin, let me touch you!"

"Teddy, *scat!*" Doc bellowed, and Teddy scatted.

Scowling, Erin pulled up the bottom of her shirt. Doc peered at the little pink bumps on her tummy.

"Chicken pox," said Mrs. Racer, and Doc agreed.

"It's not! It *can't* be!" cried Erin. "It's Cleveland, I'm sure it is. Every time he snuggles up to me I itch. Daddy, it isn't chicken pox, is it?"

Doc shook his head. "Honey, I'm an animal doctor, not a people doctor. When Vallie had chicken pox two years ago it looked a lot like this. I'm going to call Dr. O'Toole and have him check you out."

A car honked twice outside.

"That's m'son Henry," said Mrs. Racer. "I'll be here tomorrow morning, like always. Now don't you let Erin go to school, you hear, Doc? If this little girl has chicken pox, she has to stay away from all the other children so's they don't get it. And put baking soda and water on those spots. It'll stop the itching."

She bustled out, and Val jumped up and gave Erin a hug. "Maybe Dr. O'Toole will say it *is* Cleveland," she said hopefully. "But if it isn't. . . ."

"If it isn't, I won't be able to audition Saturday," Erin moaned. "And if I don't audition, I won't be the Sugarplum Fairy! And if I can't be the Sugarplum Fairy, I'll just *die*! Oh, Daddy, I don't feel sick. I'm just fine! Even if I *do* have chicken pox, I could cover up the spots with makeup or something! I wouldn't breathe on anybody, honest! I wouldn't breathe at *all*! Can't I see Dr. O'Toole *after* the audition? 'Cause if I don't definitely have chicken pox, I won't have to stay home."

"Vallie, get the baking soda," said Doc. "Erin, you're going to see the doctor tomorrow whether you like it or not. It wouldn't be fair to your classmates or to the other children at ballet school if you were contagious."

"It's not fair!" Erin cried. "It's not fair that Vallie's wish came true and mine won't just because of some dumb old spots!"

She yanked her shirt down again and sat down in a heap at the kitchen table. "This is the absolute *worst* thing that ever happened to me!" she cried.

"I know it seems bad, honey," said Doc. "But it helps sometimes to put things in perspective. There's a difference between things that are tragic, and things that are unfortunate or unlucky." He stroked her hair gently. "Now how about going upstairs with Vallie? She'll put some baking soda and water on your spots — it'll help the itching, like Mrs. Racer said. And Vallie, pop a thermometer into your sister's mouth. I don't think she has a fever, but I want to be sure. I'll call Jack O'Toole and make an appointment for tomorrow morning. Okay, Erin?"

"Okay," said Erin sadly. "But Mommy would have been so proud. . . ."

Val took Erin's hand, "Why don't I bring the TV from Dad's study into your room?" she suggested. "Thursday's a good TV night. I'll watch with you, okay?"

Erin nodded silently. Hand in hand, they went up the stairs.

An hour later, Doc came up to tuck Erin in.

"How are the itches?" he asked.

Erin made a face. "Itchy," she sighed. "I guess it isn't Cleveland after all. He hasn't been near me all night."

"That's because you hurt his feelings," said Val.

"Oh, Vallie, Cleveland couldn't understand me," Erin said.

"I'm not so sure about that," said Doc. "But it's a good thing animals don't talk back. Imagine how noisy it would be around here if they did!"

Val laughed. "I can just hear it now — Sunshine

would always be asking for more dog food, and Jocko would be yelling, 'Play with me! Play with me!' And Cleveland would say, 'Let me*owt*!' and When you let him out, he'd say, 'Let me*in*!' ''

Erin didn't smile.

Doc gave Erin a hug. "Oh, honey, I know how disappointed you are. But there was no guarantee you'd get the part no matter how hard you practiced or how much you wanted it. Not everybody can win all the time.''

"Like The Ghost," Val put in. "He didn't win every single event he entered, but he was a champion anyway. And now he'll never win anything ever again, but that's okay.''

"Those Merrills didn't think so," said Erin. "They were ready to have him *killed* just because he couldn't be a winner anymore. . . .'' She paused, then said anxiously, "I'm not like that, am I? It's not the not winning that's upset me so much — it's not being able to wear Mommy's tiara and dance the part *she* danced!''

"I know, honey," Doc said, fluffing up Erin's pillows and settling her comfortably against them. "But you have many, many dancing years ahead of you. Mommy didn't dance the Sugarplum Fairy until she was twenty, you know.''

"But twenty's so *old*!" Erin sighed.

"Ancient," Val agreed. "Hey, Erin, do you realize how lucky you are you're not a horse? Because if you were, and you were in a show, they'd have to put an 'A' after your name right now — that means you're over ten!''

That put a smile on Erin's face, even as she scratched a new spot that had suddenly popped out on her neck. Then she yawned, and Doc turned off the light, leaning down to kiss her good night.

"Good night, sleep tight," Val began.

". . . don't let the bedbugs bite," Erin finished, smiling sleepily.

As Val left Erin's room, she heard Teddy call, "Vallie? Come in a minute."

"You're supposed to be asleep," Val said, coming over to his bed. Teddy was snuggled up next to his stuffed bear, the one that had been Val's when she was little, and then was Erin's. The bear's name was Fuzzy-Wuzzy but he wasn't very fuzzy anymore. Most of his brown fur had been hugged off him long ago. "What's up?" she asked.

"I was just thinking . . . you're gonna be a vet when you grow up, like Dad, and Erin's gonna be a ballerina, like Mommy. But I don't know what *I'm* gonna be! I can't make up my mind if I want to be an astronaut, or a big-league baseball player. What do *you* think I oughta be, Vallie?"

"You know, Teddy," she said, "I don't see why you can't be *both*!"

In the glow from his night-light, Val could see a happy grin spread over her little brother's face.

"Hey, that's neat! I could be, couldn't I? I could be the first Philly astronaut!"

"Night, Teddy," said Val, straightening out his covers and tucking them in. She leaned over to kiss him, but stopped herself. Teddy had started saying kissing was "yukky."

"Aren't you going to kiss me goodnight?" he asked drowsily, clutching Fuzzy-Wuzzy closer.

Val bent down and brushed his cheek with her lips. "Good night, sleep tight . . ."

". . . don't let the bedbugs bite," Teddy mumbled against Fuzzy-Wuzzy's bald head.

Val tiptoed out.

"Aren't you ready yet, Erin?" asked Teddy, poking his head between the curtains that separated the Taylors' dining room from the living room. They weren't really curtains, just two bedsheets that Doc had hung on a clothesline, but it gave the impression of a stage.

"In a minute," came Erin's voice from the dining room. A moment later, Mrs. Racer came out from between the curtains clutching her sewing basket.

"Had to fix one of the seams on that tutu," she explained.

"I *told* you she was a fat fairy!" said Teddy, with an impish grin.

"Teddy. . . ." Doc warned. Teddy put on his "innocent angel" face.

Mrs. Racer sat down next to Val in one of the four dining room chairs that had been arranged facing the doorway. Doc was on Val's other side, and the remaining chair was reserved for Teddy, who was filling in as master of ceremonies for this very special command performance in which Miss Erin Taylor was going to dance the Sugarplum Fairy for a select audience of four.

Val bent down and picked up Cleveland, lifting him onto her lap. It was a little over three weeks since Erin had come down with chicken pox. Teddy had broken out in spots the next day, but now they were both fully recovered. Even though Erin had missed the audition, Miss Tamara had cast her as Clara, the little girl to whom the magic nutcracker is given, and had made her the understudy to the Sugarplum Fairy, since Erin knew every step of the role. Erin was pleased, but pretty sure she wouldn't have a chance to take the Fairy's place — not this Christmas, anyway. Doc had suggested today's performance and he, Val, Teddy and Mrs. Racer had joined forces to stage the production. Teddy wanted to make popcorn, like at the movies, but Erin had vetoed that idea.

"*Now?*" Teddy shouted.

"Yes — now!" Erin shouted back.

Teddy stood in front of the curtains and announced, "Ladies and gentlemen — uh, *gentleman* — the Taylor Theater is proud to present the dance of the Sugarplum Fairy, starring Miss Erin Taylor!"

Val, Doc and Mrs. Racer clapped loudly; Jocko and Sunshine barked. Teddy dashed over to the stereo and carefully lowered the needle onto Erin's record of "The Nutcracker Suite." The music, a little scratchy, but still lovely, filled the room. Teddy pulled back first one sheet, then the other, revealing Erin, a pink and silver vision in her tutu and tights with their mother's glittering tiara on her head. Teddy scurried to his chair, folding his hands in his lap.

Erin began to dance as Val and the family watched. Was this really her little sister? Val thought. She looked so much like the photographs of their mother in the same role. Suddenly Teddy poked Val in the ribs. "She isn't really fat," he whispered in her ear. "I just said that to make her mad."

"I know," Val whispered back. "It would be nice if you told her that afterwards."

"Maybe I will . . . and then, maybe I won't," said Teddy, under his breath.

"*Teddy!*" Doc hissed, reaching over and tapping him lightly on the shoulder.

119

Erin was right, Val thought, smiling. Mom would have been very proud!

After Erin's recital was over and she'd been hugged and congratulated by everyone, there was a knock at the front door. Val hurried to answer it. When she opened the door, she saw Toby standing there looking sheepish. Erin had invited him to come to the performance, but Toby had mumbled something about having to help his father and brothers at the dairy. Val had suggested that he might drop in for the celebration afterward, and he'd said that he might, especially when he heard that Mrs. Racer would be making her super chocolate-chip cookies.

"Hi," said Toby. "Just finished helping Dad with the cows. Uh . . . I brought something for Erin."

He shoved a bunch of roses at Val.

"They're from my mom's garden. She said that's what you give a ballerina after the show."

"Oh, Toby, they're beautiful!" cried Erin, scooting around Val and taking the bouquet. "I'm so glad you came! Come on in — we have ice cream and cookies." She did a pirouette on her toes and ran off to find her father. "Daddy! Guess what! I got my very first bouquet!"

It was warm for October—unseasonably warm, the weathermen said on radio and television. It was like an extended summer. Some of the trees had started to turn from their brilliant green to shades of yellow, orange, and red, but the sun was shining brightly and the air felt like spring. Val was astride The Ghost for the very first time, and they were ambling down a country lane. Overhead, the leaves were changing and every now and then one would spiral down like a feather from some exotic bird. The Ghost tossed his head and pranced like a colt — it was as if he felt the promise of fall in the air, and he'd been penned up for so long that he couldn't help dancing. Just like Erin, Val thought. She thought of a poem her English class had read not too long ago — about how you couldn't tell the dancer from the dance. Val liked that. It was true for Erin, and for The Ghost.

Beneath her, she felt The Ghost's powerful muscles moving. The sun was shining, filtering down dappled, like The Ghost's gray coat, to bless them both.

Val said aloud, "I'm the happiest girl in the world. And you're the most wonderful horse there is!" The Ghost's ears flicked back and forth, as though he knew exactly what she'd said. Val leaned over and patted his sleek shoulder, warm and silken beneath her hand. "I know you can't see how beautiful everything is," she told the horse, "but take my word for it — it's wonderful! And one day soon, you'll see it, too! We'll have plenty of good times together, Ghost. 'Cause I'm going to make sure that you are always just as happy as you make me!"

Look for the next book in the Animal Inn series,
A Kid's Best Friend, coming soon!

But what about the dog? Where on Earth was
the van?

Just then she saw it coming down Orchard
Lane, and Val ran to open the front door. The van
screeched to a stop, and Mike Strickler scrambled
out. He flung open the side door of the van, and
Toby emerged, staggering under the weight of a
huge collie. The dog lay limp in his arms, its gold-
and-white fur stained with blood.

Val gasped, and stood aside as Toby came in
with his burden. Toby's usually cheerful face was
grim, his brown hair falling over his worried eyes.

"Oh, the poor thing!" cried Mrs. Starner. "Is he
dead?" Her dog, Fritz, began to bark.

"Not yet," Toby mumbled.

America's Favorite Series

THE BABY-SITTERS CLUB®

by Ann M. Martin

Collect Them All!

The seven girls at Stoneybrook Middle School get into all kinds of adventures...with school, boys, and, of course, baby-sitting!